Captured in Ink

Also From Carrie Ann Ryan

The Montgomery Ink: Fort Collins Series:
Book 1: *Inked Persuasion*
Book 2: *Inked Obsession*
Book 3: *Inked Devotion*

The Promise Me Series:
Book 1: *Forever Only Once*
Book 2: *From That Moment*
Book 3: *Far From Destined*
Book 4: *From Our First*

The On My Own Series:
Book 1: *My One Night*
Book 2: *My Rebound*
Book 3: *My Next Play*

The Tattered Royals Series:
Book 1: *Royal Line*

The Ravenwood Coven Series:
Book 1: *Dawn Unearthed*

Montgomery Ink:
Book 0.5: *Ink Inspired*
Book 0.6: *Ink Reunited*
Book 1: *Delicate Ink*
Book 1.5: *Forever Ink*
Book 2: *Tempting Boundaries*
Book 4: *Harder than Words*
Book 4: *Written in Ink*
Book 4.5: *Hidden Ink*
Book 5: *Ink Enduring*
Book 6: *Ink Exposed*
Book 6.5: *Adoring Ink*
Book 6.6 *Love, Honor, and Ink*
Book 7: *Inked Expressions*
Book 7.3: *Dropout*

Redwood Pack Series:
Book 1: *An Alpha's Path*
Book 2: *A Taste for a Mate*
Book 3: *Trinity Bound*
Book 3.5: *A Night Away*
Book 4: *Enforcer's Redemption*
Book 4.5: *Blurred Expectations*
Book 4.7: *Forgiveness*
Book 5: *Shattered Emotions*
Book 6: *Hidden Destiny*
Book 6.5: *A Beta's Haven*
Book 7: *Fighting Fate*
Book 7.5: *Loving the Omega*
Book 7.7: *The Hunted Heart*
Book 8: *Wicked Wolf*

The Talon Pack:
Book 1: *Tattered Loyalties*
Book 2: *An Alpha's Choice*
Book 3: *Mated in Mist*
Book 4: *Wolf Betrayed*
Book 5: *Fractured Silence*
Book 6: *Destiny Disgraced*
Book 7: *Eternal Mourning*
Book 8: *Strength Enduring*
Book 9: *Forever Broken*

The Elements of Five Series:
Book 1: *From Breath and Ruin*
Book 2: *From Flame and Ash*
Book 3: *From Spirit and Binding*
Book 4: *From Shadow and Silence*

The Branded Pack Series:
(Written with Alexandra Ivy)
Book 1: *Stolen and Forgiven*
Book 2: *Abandoned and Unseen*
Book 3: *Buried and Shadowed*

Captured in Ink

A Montgomery Ink: Boulder Novella

By Carrie Ann Ryan

1001 DARK NIGHTS

PRESS

Captured in Ink
A Montgomery Ink: Boulder Novella
By Carrie Ann Ryan

1001 Dark Nights

Copyright 2021 Carrie Ann Ryan
ISBN: 978-1-951812-29-4

Foreword: Copyright 2014 M. J. Rose

Published by 1001 Dark Nights Press, an imprint of Evil Eye Concepts, Incorporated

Sign up for the 1001 Dark Nights Newsletter
and be entered to win a Tiffany Key necklace.

There's a contest every month!

Go to www.1001DarkNights.com to subscribe.

**As a bonus, all subscribers can download
FIVE FREE exclusive books!**

Acknowledgments from the Author

I adore writing in the Montgomery Ink world and when I get a chance to also work with 1,001 Dark Nights, I know I'm going to be blessed.

Thank you, Liz, Jillian, and MJ for believing in me and letting me play around with characters I might not have been able to write before!

Thank you Chelle for being my touchstone and best friend. My books are better because of you.

Thank you, Julia Kent for letting me borrow you for a very steamy menage romance. Haha.

And thank you, dear readers for following me for this long. I can't wait to see where we go!

One Thousand and One Dark Nights

Once upon a time, in the future…

*I was a student fascinated with stories and learning.
I studied philosophy, poetry, history, the occult, and
the art and science of love and magic. I had a vast
library at my father's home and collected thousands
of volumes of fantastic tales.*

*I learned all about ancient races and bygone
times. About myths and legends and dreams of all
people through the millennium. And the more I read
the stronger my imagination grew until I discovered
that I was able to travel into the stories… to actually
become part of them.*

*I wish I could say that I listened to my teacher
and respected my gift, as I ought to have. If I had, I
would not be telling you this tale now.
But I was foolhardy and confused, showing off
with bravery.*

*One afternoon, curious about the myth of the
Arabian Nights, I traveled back to ancient Persia to
see for myself if it was true that every day Shahryar
(Persian: شهریار, "king") married a new virgin, and then
sent yesterday's wife to be beheaded. It was written
and I had read that by the time he met Scheherazade,
the vizier's daughter, he'd killed one thousand
women.*

Something went wrong with my efforts. I arrived in the midst of the story and somehow exchanged places with Scheherazade — a phenomena that had never occurred before and that still to this day, I cannot explain.

Now I am trapped in that ancient past. I have taken on Scheherazade's life and the only way I can protect myself and stay alive is to do what she did to protect herself and stay alive.

Every night the King calls for me and listens as I spin tales. And when the evening ends and dawn breaks, I stop at a point that leaves him breathless and yearning for more. And so the King spares my life for one more day, so that he might hear the rest of my dark tale.

As soon as I finish a story... I begin a new one... like the one that you, dear reader, have before you now.

Chapter 1

Ronin

As soon as our guests left, I knew I would bend my wife over our dining room table and finish what we started before we were interrupted.

Julia looked at me over her wine glass, her blue eyes dancing with laughter. Oh, I had a feeling she knew exactly where my mind had gone. Was it my fault, though? Honestly? She might be wearing a dress that covered her completely and went down to her knees, but it hugged her curves, and all I wanted to do was ruck it up her hips and see what we could get up to. We experimented often and tried everything we could to fulfill our needs and changing desires. I'd found my perfect partner, and I fell in love with her more every day.

She rolled her eyes, and I gulped half my wine, trying to calm myself. As it was, my dick pressed into my jeans, and I held back a curse.

Julia's coworker and his two spouses were telling a story about one of their family members, and I was only half listening. Julia was laughing along, paying attention, and I knew I should, as well.

I liked Ethan Montgomery and his spouses, Holland and Lincoln. They were great people, and I got along with them. I even worked with their brother-in-law, Marcus, at the library. We were all one big tattooed family—and admittedly a little weird. And yet all I could think about was my wife.

I still couldn't believe I had married the love of my life, and that she still wanted to be with me after all these years.

"Are you going to keep making swoony eyes at Julia over the table, or are you going to start paying attention to us?" Lincoln asked, and I cleared my throat as everyone at the table broke out into laughter.

"Sorry, it's been a strange day." I shook my head and took another sip of my wine.

"I vaguely remember Marcus saying you had book club today," Holland said, her voice kind. She owned a touristy shop that sold art and other exclusive pieces down the street from the library. I had gotten Julia's birthday gift from her, and I knew when the holidays came up, I'd probably be shopping there again. It didn't hurt that Lincoln sold a couple of his art pieces through the store, although his work was so sought after these days, it was hard to keep them in the shop. With some of them going for thousands, if not more, it didn't make sense security-wise to keep them in her small store.

I loved that my friends were all connected and settling down. The Montgomerys, in particular, had been through a lot recently, and it was good to see them happy for once. There was talk of babies and future plans and the like. I smiled over at Julia again as Ethan began talking about work and an upcoming trip, and I wondered when we would start that next phase of our relationship. We both wanted children and had talked about it in the past, but we were taking our time. We still had more to do in our lives before we took that next step, but it would probably be a good idea to at least bring it up so we were on the same page.

I had learned long ago from one disastrous relationship after another that without true communication, things could get fucked up faster than you could blink. And I would do everything in my power to never hurt Julia.

"You're not going on this work trip?" I asked Ethan, trying to get my head back into the conversation.

Both Julia and Ethan were computational chemists, with Julia focused on data analysis. However, she worked with Ethan on most projects. Both of them were way above my pay grade when it came to understanding science, but I liked learning new things. Hence why, after I left the military, I became a librarian, something the exact opposite of what my initial career had been. Some people might not quite understand why, but it was books for me, and that's all I needed. That, and Julia.

"No, they only need Julia and another member of our team. I offered to go in her place because I know you have an anniversary coming up, but she's the one who spearheaded this, you know?" Ethan added.

Julia just shook her head. "We did it together, thank you very much.

You were just as big a part of this project as I was. But you know Jeff, he wanted to go because the event is in Vegas, so it was either you or me and the guy in charge."

I ground my teeth. "I don't like this Jeff guy."

Julia shrugged. "He's not that bad. He's brilliant, and he's always quite nice. And he isn't one of those guys who thinks that because I'm a woman, I don't know how to do science or come up with my own proofs. But he's also in a higher position than us, and if he wants to go on a trip where he will get his work done but also party? He's going to go."

"Yeah, he's not a jerk," Ethan put in. "And he did do work on the project. So, it's not like there's any bad blood."

"I still don't have to like him," I said, lifting my chin.

Julia just snorted. "Of course not, honey. You can hate him all you want."

"I heard that placating tone," I said dryly.

"It wasn't like I was hiding it."

"You two are way too cute." Holland smiled broadly as she looked between us.

I grinned. "Thank you. We try."

"I still can't believe it's been over a year since I met you guys," Holland put in. "I feel like it was just yesterday that I was coming into Ethan's life and meeting you. And now look at us, everybody's married and happy, and we're all grown up."

"It was quite an experience the first time we saw you," Lincoln said dryly.

"That *was* quite a memorable way to meet," Ethan added.

I smiled. "I don't know what I would've done if I'd met Julia while she was in a big wedding dress, drinking wine out of a paper bag."

Holland just rolled her eyes. "It was a bottle of wine in a paper bag. It's not like I poured it into the bag."

Ethan snorted. "I like how that's what you get upset about."

Holland grinned. "It was good wine. And I know they make good boxed wine now, but I just think it would've been worse if I was sitting there drinking out of a box or a true bag."

"I stand corrected," I said, and we all laughed again.

"How did you two meet?" Lincoln asked. "I just realized I don't know."

I looked over at Julia and held out my arm. She slid her hand into mine and squeezed it. "Over a book, of course," I said, and she smiled.

"I went into the library to pick up some reading material for work, things that are hard to find online. And, over the books, I met a man who growled at me and told me I wasn't allowed to take them away from the library."

"I didn't growl," I corrected her.

"You growled. But I found it kind of hot."

I winked. "Okay, then I growled."

She laughed as I wanted her to, and I just followed the long lines of her neck with my gaze and imagined my mouth on her skin. *Soon*, I promised myself. I'd wrap that long, chestnut hair around my fist and have my way with her.

We'd have to go at it a little differently tonight than usual. Mostly because my leg hurt, but that's what happened after another day of PT and getting fitted for my new prosthesis. I ached, but I would still have fun with my wife. That was why I was doing all of this. To have a life worth living.

"See? That's a wonderful story. And not as dramatic as mine," Holland said dryly.

"It's good to have entertaining meet-cutes," Julia put in, squeezing my hand before she went back to her wine. "Even if they seem subtle at first, they'll always be memories."

"Is it weird that I don't remember the first time I met Lincoln?" Ethan asked.

Lincoln shook his head. "No, but I remember. I think. I feel like you've always been in my life, though."

I chuckled as Julia and Holland both let out *aw* sounds. "See what you did? You just beat us all in the romance department."

"I can't help it, it's the way I roll," Lincoln said, grinning.

"You are so going to get lucky later." Ethan winked, and Julia snorted.

"See, you went for sweet, and you just got perverted," Julia said.

"Should I not have?" Ethan asked, his face serious. "I know we're coworkers and all, is this wrong?"

Julia shook her head. "You're at our home with your spouses, we're going to joke. I promise. And you're never inappropriate at work. You're fine."

"I still worry."

"And that's why you're Ethan Montgomery. You're a worrier."

We continued talking for a bit longer and then cleared the table before the triad left. I knew they didn't get out very often unless it was to go to a family member's house or a friend's. They did go out on dates in public, but they usually did their own thing at home or came over to our place or someone else's. While the world had changed, not everybody agreed with their relationship. I had once been in a triad myself. It hadn't lasted, and while my heart still ached a little thinking about it, I remembered the fierce looks from those who watched.

It hadn't been easy to be in that relationship, and I knew that it would never be okay for some people. As long as there was open communication and true love and attraction between the triad, it could work. But some things had to be given up to have that relationship. I was so happy for Ethan, Holland, and Lincoln. Their life was never going to be as easy as a heterosexual relationship in some respects, but they were making it work.

"What has you all serious?" Julia asked, running her knuckles along my chin. I looked down at her, love piercing my heart. Every time I looked at her, I thought of our future, our past, and everything we held in our present. I had once taken what love could be for granted, and I did not want to be that person again. And so, with my relationship with Julia, I did everything I could to show her that I loved her, and that we were meant to be.

I leaned down and kissed her softly, moaning as I wrapped my arms around her. She sank into me, deepening the kiss, and I groaned.

"I'm going to ask you again, what has you all serious?"

I sighed and rested my head on top of hers for a moment before pushing away to lean back against the counter. "I was just thinking about how having a triad relationship takes a little more work, and how Ethan and the loves of his life can't go out to every restaurant they want and that they have to be cognizant of the people around them."

Julia frowned but nodded. "You're right. They do. A lot of people when seeing three people at a restaurant will just think that maybe it's a couple and their friend. But if they want to hold hands or even kiss in the parking lot as they get into their cars, they have to be aware. It was the same way with Sasha and me. I couldn't go out with her to a restaurant without being aware of our surroundings the way you and I can go out."

"I hate that that's even an issue."

"It's so much better than it used to be. My ex and I had our share of problems, ones that we are not going to get into tonight, but Sasha wanted to face the world head-on, and so we did. And I'll always be grateful for that. Because I got to experience dating for real, and I was never hidden in a closet somewhere."

"And then you met me, and everything is perfect now," I said, trying to lighten the mood.

She snorted, shaking her head. "I know you were in a triad once, you and Kincaid and Alexis. Was it the same as it is with Ethan and them? Did you guys go out on dates, or did you hide?"

I froze at the mention of Kincaid and Alexis. It was only natural that I'd be thinking of my personal triad from the past, considering that we'd just had dinner with a triad that reminded me of my first long-term relationship. It was just weird to have it mentioned so out in the open. I did not have secrets from Julia, nor did she from me. It was how we made what we had work.

Still, it wasn't easy to think about.

"We didn't go out much," I said honestly. "It sucks. Alexis was hiding us from her family, and while Kincaid and I were completely open, we got in a few fights with others over it. So, we usually ended up just going out as couples and doing our triad thing at home. It sucked. Though there were many reasons our relationship didn't work. That was only one of them."

The main reason was that they had left me. But I didn't want to think about that.

Julia cupped my face.

"I'm sorry, baby. I didn't mean to bring up such bad things. I love you."

I leaned down and kissed her again.

"I love you, too. And as for Ethan, Holland, and Lincoln… They aren't like my old relationship. They do go out as a triad. They're just careful about it like most people aware of their safety are. Other people just need to get over it," I said, laughing.

"They're always safe at our home."

"Hell yeah, they are."

I kissed her again, leaning into her, and she wrapped her arms around me, her hands going to my back, her nails digging in. I groaned at the sensation and leaned forward, kissing her harder.

My leg ached, and I pulled away a bit, shaking my head. "I should sit."

A shadow crossed her face, and I knew it was because she didn't like seeing me in pain. I hated feeling weak in front of her, but that was something we were dealing with. Albeit slowly.

She led me into the living room, and I sat down, and she straddled my waist. She didn't even sit down on me, simply hovered over me, and I didn't mind. She'd be sitting on me soon enough, and we'd have a lot more fun then. I slid my hands up her back, enjoying how her dress gathered around her hips. And then I let my fingers dance along her skin before moving down to her panties and playing with the seam.

"You know this is a very tiny little piece of lace that you're wearing under here."

"I figured it'd be easier for you to finger fuck me," she said with a wink.

I groaned, lifting my hips to press against her heat. "I'm going to do more than finger fuck you."

She smiled at me and then kissed me hard, both of us groaning as I pulled her dress up higher, then cupped her breasts over her bra. She rocked on my hips, and both of us whimpered, my need for her growing each time she rubbed against me and the sensations it caused.

I nearly pulled her panties to the side and had her help me with my pants, but I wanted more time. Needed more time.

The doorbell rang, and we both froze, panting.

"Do you think they forgot something?" she asked, her voice low and husky and filled with desire.

I swallowed hard, my hands shaking. "I hope to hell they're quick. And if it's someone trying to sell us something at this time of night? I'm going to have to kill them."

She snorted and scrambled up. "I've got it."

I shook my head. "Like I said, at this time of night? I'm going with you." I levered myself off the couch and followed her. She made it to the door before me, looked through the peephole, and frowned.

"I don't recognize him."

"Him?" I asked, the hair on the back of my neck standing on end.

She opened the door before I could say anything, and I blinked, staring at the man from my past, the one who had just been in my thoughts earlier. I wanted to close the door in his face and pretend that this portal into memories long past didn't exist.

I could feel Julia freeze in front of me, but I knew she didn't recognize him. She had never even seen a photo of this man.

But from the way Kincaid stared at me, I knew she likely had a good idea exactly who he was.

"Ronin," Kincaid said, his voice that low, bear-like growl that had once sent me into oblivion. He looked rough, his red hair curling over his forehead, his beard bushy. There were blond streaks in it now as if he had been out in the sun, his freckles popping on his nose. He wore a T-shirt so I could see his ink, newer designs that I had never touched before, and older ones that I had once licked.

And here he was, in front of me, the man who had walked away without a word, and yet he was on my doorstep as if nothing had happened.

"Kincaid," I whispered, and Julia froze again.

The man I had loved, the guy that I promised I would never love again was standing in front of my wife and me.

The world crashed down around me.

Chapter 2

Kincaid

I'd made a mistake. Another damn misstep that would haunt me.

I glanced at the woman with the dark hair, bright blue eyes, and a pouting mouth that made my throat go dry, and yet, right at that moment, I only had eyes for the man standing behind her.

Ronin.

He was here, so close to me, and yet so far away. My fault. Always my fault. But he was *so* close.

Memories of years gone by flooded me, and all I wanted to do was reach for him, hold him close, and forget everything that had happened in the past. But that wouldn't happen. It couldn't.

Because as I looked at Ronin, I knew there would never be forgiveness in that gaze.

But that wasn't the only thing. No. I finally glanced at the woman in front of me again, noticed the ring on her finger, saw the matching one on Ronin's, and knew I was too late. Years too late.

I had spent too long trying to dig myself out of the darkness, attempting to claw my way out of horror, and I had missed my chance at something more. *My fault*, I repeated to myself—all my fault.

"Kincaid?" the woman in front of me asked, her voice soft. "It's good to finally meet you," she said, although her voice was devoid of emotion. I didn't know if she was lying or not.

I rolled my shoulders back. "I'm sorry for disturbing you so late. I just got into town. I'll let you be. Sorry about this." I turned to walk away, to let the pain ease ever so slightly even though I knew it never would, but a small hand grabbed my arm—the strength of the grip surprising me. I looked down at that diamond ring that had been put on her finger by the man I once loved. The man I still loved? I wasn't sure.

"Come inside. Please."

"I don't think that would be a good idea," I said.

Ronin didn't say anything. And, somehow, that hurt worse than him yelling at me and throwing me out. But I would deserve it if he did. I deserved all of it.

"I'm Julia. Please, come inside. It's late and getting a bit chilly. You don't even have a coat on."

"I'm fine," I said.

"Please. You don't want me to get mean." Her eyes twinkled as I peered at her face.

This was the woman Ronin had married, and I liked her. She was firm, smiled, and looked like she would take no shit—the perfect partner for Ronin. She was so different from Alexis. I could already tell that, and maybe that was a good thing. She likely wouldn't run away when things got tough.

Though I had no idea how I could tell that from a single touch, a momentary glance.

"Come on. Ronin and I were just cleaning up after dinner."

That's when I finally noticed the swollen lips—the tousled hair.

Oh, they had definitely been doing something after dinner, but it wasn't cleaning up.

Jealousy slashed at me, but I pushed it away.

I deserved this, and so much more.

Finally, I looked at Ronin again, saw the longing mixed with anger in his gaze, and knew I couldn't just leave. I would after, but I couldn't hurt this woman, not when I knew if I walked away, I would only leave ashes in my wake for her to deal with. And neither of them deserved that.

"Okay, just for a moment."

Relief and fear slid through Julia's gaze, but she blinked it away quickly. She seemed so strong. I couldn't help but like her immediately.

I followed her inside the modest home that these two had made together. It was all white lines with dark furniture and trees and art on the wall. I liked it. I could see some influences of Ronin, the man I had known before. As well as some more feminine tastes that had to have come from Julia.

They had somehow melded and created a life together. And I wasn't part of it. Maybe if I hadn't run away—but no, there was no taking that back. And I hadn't been the man who was in love with Ronin for a long time. It wouldn't have mattered if I had come back any sooner. I hadn't been ready—as selfish as that was.

"Can I get you something to drink? We still have an open bottle of wine. Our friends were over for dinner, and it's been a nice evening."

I knew Julia was rambling, and yet Ronin wasn't saying a damn word.

"I'm okay. Thank you. I need to drive."

"Oh, okay. Any water?"

"I'm fine. Thank you for welcoming me into your home."

Her eyes warmed, but then she stood at Ronin's side, her hand sliding into his. Her loyalties were with her husband, as they should be. And Ronin was hurting. That much was clear. If the other man didn't say something soon, I wouldn't just be walking out of here, Julia would be *pushing* me out. That much I knew.

I cleared my throat. "I just got back into town, and this was the last address I had of yours," I whispered.

"I sent you a letter when I moved in," Ronin said, his voice wooden. "Before Julia and I even got married. I didn't know you got the letter. But, apparently, you did since you had the address."

"I read your letter. Letter*s*," I corrected, my voice hollow.

Julia looked between us, tension clearly riding her. But hell, it was riding all of us.

The man I had once loved narrowed his eyes. "Didn't want to write back?"

"I couldn't, Ronin." And that was the truth, but not all of it.

"Sure. I can see that. I'm here. Same place I've been for a long damn while. What? Ten years now? And where have you been? Trotting the globe?"

"There were things I needed to do, Ronin."

"Good to know. Did you get them done? Or maybe you don't need to tell me. You didn't tell me much even then."

"I can see this was a mistake," I said quickly.

"You're pretty good at making those, aren't you?" Ronin bit out.

"I think I'm the one who made a mistake by allowing him in." Julia moved forward.

Ronin shook his head, and I swallowed hard. The other man looked over at his wife, cupped her cheek, and lowered his forehead to hers. That pang of jealousy hit hard again, and I swallowed back any emotions that might drown me. The love between them was palpable. I almost felt like I could reach out and touch it.

There was so much trust and understanding in that bond. It was something I had thought I had with him until I had to go away. I hadn't been able to understand it at the time, had been too scared of so many things, and Ronin had gotten hurt because of it.

"No, you didn't do anything wrong. I'm sorry for making you feel that way," Ronin whispered.

I felt like I was intruding, even if this *was* about me. And yet, was it? No, it had to be about Ronin. That was the thing. It needed to be about him after so many years of hiding from it.

I cleared my throat. "I didn't know you were married," I whispered. "I shouldn't have come. If I had known, I wouldn't be here."

Ronin turned to me, his eyes dark. "And then I still wouldn't know if you were alive or dead."

He had no idea how close to the mark his words were, and yet I couldn't open my mouth and tell him. Not now. I needed to. I knew that. That was the whole point of me being here. Still, I couldn't. Not yet.

"Should I let you two be?" Julia asked, looking between us.

What kind of woman was this that she had the strength and capacity to leave her husband alone with his former lover? I didn't know this Julia, but I wanted to. And maybe that should scare me, but it didn't.

I liked her, even if I was jealous of her. But that was my problem, not hers.

"I came here to talk to you, Ronin. To apologize. To tell you everything. But maybe I should just go. It's only going to hurt everything."

Ronin ran his hands through his hair, pushing it back from his face. It was longer than it had been when we were together, and I liked it. He had ink on his body, and I could tell from the way he stood that his leg hurt him. We'd gotten together soon after the IED blast had taken off his leg in Afghanistan. I had been with him when he was first learning to be himself again, and I could still read his face and know when he was in pain. He had grown into an even more beautiful man—and I had missed him.

I hated that I'd hurt him.

"Why did you go?" Ronin asked. "Why did you leave without a word, other than saying it was over and leaving a note? Just tell me that, and then you can go. I hate unknowns."

"You're a librarian, you always did love research and discovering answers."

Ronin snorted. "That's not the same. I couldn't look up anything to find out what the fuck happened to you."

"Let's sit down," Julia said. "I was going to leave to give you two some space, but I don't think I can do that. Is it okay if I'm here when you say your piece?" Julia asked, looking directly into my face.

I liked this woman. "Of course. You two seem perfect for each other."

"We are," Ronin ground out.

I ignored the barb, even though I knew I'd earned it. "I'll take that seat," I said then let out a breath. "Plus, I guess you shouldn't be on your feet after, what? PT today?"

Ronin narrowed his eyes. "Stop acting as if you know me. It's been far too long for that."

Ronin turned on his heel and made his way to the couch. He sat down as if he had no pain, and then leaned forward, putting his forearms on his thighs. "Talk."

Julia sat next to him, rubbing his back, even as she looked at me. I swallowed hard and took the chair across the coffee table from them and let out a breath.

"After Alexis left us, both of us were broken. We weren't talking like we used to."

"Yes, but I figured we'd talk it out eventually," Roman bit out.

"Ronin, let him speak."

He glared at Julia before softening his expression and nodding.

"You're right. The more I interrupt, the longer he's going to be here."

Julia rolled her eyes and gave me a look. We shared something in that moment, though I couldn't quite name it. And I didn't know how I felt about it. Given the way she shook her head and pulled away slightly, I had a feeling she was on the same page as I was.

Odd.

"I took that job, the one where it should have been safe."

"Ronin said you were a photojournalist?" Julia asked, her voice soft again.

"I used to be. Now, I do photography for myself and my business. I don't go to war-torn countries anymore. I don't put myself in the heat of battle. Not after the accident."

Ronin's gaze shot up.

"What accident?"

"Pretty similar to yours. We rolled over an IED, blew our Jeep to hell and back."

Ronin's face blanched. "Ours?"

I nodded tightly, my gut roiling, bile filling my throat. "Sophia and I took the job together. Mom and Dad weren't happy because they didn't want their kids in high-risk situations. They wanted her to be a reporter for a local newspaper and talk about the largest pumpkin or whatever was going on with Main Street. Instead, she took a job with *The Chronicle* and was doing an AP report for the area. We were a team and worked together."

"Oh, Kincaid," Julia whispered, and I had a feeling she knew where I was going with this.

"I was out of it for nearly two weeks by the time I woke up and heard that she didn't make it. Sophia died on impact. Didn't even make it out of the fucking Jeep. I broke my leg, my arm, had a skull fracture, second and third-degree burns down my back. But I survived. Sophia didn't. Took me a long time to get home, and it took me a hell of a long time to pull myself out of the bottle."

Ronin's eyes widened, and I nodded tightly. "I'm an alcoholic. I've been sober for three years, two months, and six days. I didn't contact you or write back or do anything because I blamed myself. I'm figuring out who I am again, but I came here to apologize and to tell you. I don't plan on drinking today or tomorrow. Only I'm not the same person I was. I lost Sophia, on a job that I was asked to do, something I got my sister into. No matter how many steps I take to get out of the bottle, I'm still going to hate the way I treated you and what happened to Sophia. I don't fully know why I'm here. I just figured you ought to know."

I stood up then, ready to leave, but then Ronin did the same, Julia right beside him.

"Jesus Christ, Kincaid," Ronin bit out. And then he was at my side, tugging me close. I slammed into his chest and froze for a moment before I wrapped my arms around him and lowered my head to his shoulder. The tears came, and a jagged sob ripped through me. My shirt was wet, and I knew Ronin was crying right along with me. Then there was a small hand on my back, rubbing my shirt, and I knew the other was doing the same to Ronin's. Julia stood between us, and I held her close, too, needing the comfort of this stranger, something I hadn't even known I needed. And then Ronin wrapped his arms around his wife, rested his head against hers, and looked up at me.

"You're home," Ronin said.

I swallowed hard. "Doesn't feel like it yet. But I'm working on it."

The two of them held each other close, and I took a step back, one I hoped they didn't notice.

Because while there might be forgiveness in Ronin's eyes—even though I didn't think he'd ever truly get there—I knew I had come here for more than just that reason.

And I would never get what I wanted.

The man that I loved more than anything held his wife close, and I realized there was no way I would step between that. There was no way I would break that bond and connection.

I had lost everything once before.

And now, I was looking at what I could have had if I hadn't broken.

Once again, I had failed.

Once again, I was the mistake.

And I could only blame myself for it.

Chapter 3

Julia

"He just showed up?" Holland asked as she moved a picture frame to another part of the shelf.

I nodded, dusting behind her. I didn't work at her shop, but I couldn't just stand around and do nothing while she worked. And because I tended to wring my hands or bother her with my nervous ticks, she generally gave me something to organize or handed me something to clean with while I was there. Not because she needed the help, but because she knew *I* needed to calm down.

I liked Ethan's wife, and I was glad that I'd become closer to him and his family over time. Close enough that I felt free to talk to Holland about Kincaid and Ronin and what'd happened when my husband's ex-boyfriend came to town.

"Is Ronin okay?" Holland asked, continuing to organize while I dusted.

"He says he is. But he's closed off."

"Does he tend to do that when things happen? Big things?" Holland frowned. "I keep asking you weird new questions. But I think it's more that I know you, but I don't know Ronin all that well. I don't know how he usually reacts to things. Probably because he just rolls with the punches and tends to act as if nothing's wrong when I'm around him."

I smiled at that. "Well, that's Ronin. He keeps everything inside himself and pretends that nothing is wrong so he can take care of everybody else. He usually shares his feelings with me, but right now, he's hiding everything, and I don't know what to do about that."

"What do you think is hurting him more right now?" Holland asked, her voice low.

No one else was in the store since the place hadn't opened quite yet. But soon, the tourists would be in, coming in droves, and I would leave Holland to it so she could get to work and not have my problems bothering her. It was nice to have a friend to talk to, though. I wasn't very good at opening up to people. Ronin had been the first person I'd truly bared myself to and found my place.

"Sometimes, I have to dig things out of him, but he opens for me. Honestly, I think he feels guilty. Guilt over hating Kincaid all this time, thinking the man left him for reasons that were all on Ronin, and not things that were so extraordinary and out of his control."

"And it's not just the two of them. And not you," Holland added.

I winced. "Ronin doesn't talk about Alexis much. Hell, he doesn't even talk about Kincaid often, and I know we need to talk about him. As for Alexis? She just didn't fit with them. And I know they tried a permanent triad like the three of you have, but it didn't work out. In the end, Alexis cheated and left them."

Holland's eyes widened. "She cheated?"

"Yes, and it was horrible. Ronin has always been very timid—or at least untrusting—when it comes to forming new attachments because of it. It took us a while to figure out who we were to each other because I have my own issues, and he needed to get over his. I thought we had made it past that, but Alexis hurt him, then Kincaid broke him."

My voice cracked at the end of that statement, and I shook my head when Holland reached out. "I'm sorry. I'm fine. I just need to talk to him. I think we need to work it out first."

"I know Ronin loves you. You do, too. Yes, you should talk to him. Figure out what he wants."

I bit my lip. "I don't know what I should do."

Holland shook her head. "I don't know either. But you are his wife, you took vows. You two need to talk and figure out what you both want. Kincaid came back. Maybe to apologize, or perhaps for Ronin himself. But that's not how things are going to work."

"You're right. I'm not going to walk away," I said on a laugh that held little humor. "But I do need to work out what Ronin wants."

"And you, too," Holland said softly. "You need to dig into what you're feeling also."

I swallowed hard and did my best to change the subject to babies and weddings that had nothing to do with me. I needed time to think, and I had to talk with my husband.

* * * *

By the time I made it home, people were out and about, running their errands, and I felt a little bit better about what I needed to do. I pulled into the driveway, parked, and looked at the home we had made together. Ronin had bought it for himself after the relationship with Alexis and Kincaid took its turn. Ronin needed a one-story home because stairs weren't easy on his prosthesis, and frankly, I didn't mind. Although I loved the look of some two-story homes against the backdrop of the Rocky Mountains, a nice ranch-style home was perfect for me after long days where I wanted to curl up next to my husband and remember that I was blessed in some ways, even if the horrors of some things never truly went away.

"Baby?" Ronin asked from the side of the car. I started, realizing my window was open.

"Crap. I need to close the window, and then I'm coming inside."

He frowned, reached forward, and rubbed his knuckle against my cheek. I leaned into him, craving his touch. "Are you okay?"

"I don't know," I said honestly, letting out a breath.

His eyes darkened a bit, and then he nodded. "Let's get you inside. I think we have a few things to talk about."

Dread and something else turned inside me. We needed to discuss things. That's what we did in our relationship. The first thing he had told me when we started dating was that for the two of us to work, we needed to have open communication.

It wasn't always easy to bare yourself to another, but honesty was the best, and it worked for us. And that meant I needed to be completely honest with Ronin.

I got the window up and made my way into the house, moving into Ronin's space as we walked together.

"Need me to make you a drink?" Ronin asked.

"You mean like a bloody Mary? It's like not even noon yet."

My husband smiled and leaned forward, brushing my lips with his. "I love you, Julia."

Tears pricked the backs of my eyes, and I wrapped my arms around his waist and kissed him soundly. "I love you too, husband."

"Let's take a seat, and then I guess we should talk."

I nodded and walked to the living room. I sank onto the couch, letting the cushions envelop me. Ronin sat next to me, his thick thigh pressing against mine. I loved the feeling of him touching me, the heat of him. He had dark eyes and darker hair and had filled out even more after he left the military. He was all muscles, his upper body built. Not as built as Kincaid, but very muscular.

I didn't know why that thought even entered my mind, but I pushed it away. At least for now.

"You've been quiet," I said suddenly, and Ronin nodded.

"I've had to get over a lot of misconceptions I'm trying to trace back to my past. I was so wrong about a lot of things, and I hate that."

I nodded and tangled my fingers with his. "Kincaid looks like he's been through hell but has come out the other side." I let out a breath. "And he came here for you," I whispered.

Ronin froze. "He might've come here for me, but seeing as I'm married, it doesn't matter. Does it?"

I didn't answer and put that thought aside for the moment. "After Kincaid told us everything that happened with his sister and him getting hurt, we all hugged, and then he left. He gave us his number, but we didn't promise we'd see him again or anything. I need to know what's going to happen."

My voice broke again, and I hated that I was crying over this. My husband looked so sad, broken once again over a man that he had loved. And I didn't know how to fix it. I remembered Kincaid, recalled the way he looked as if he had glimpsed happiness once again, only for it to be taken away from him. The man had lost so much. From the stories Ronin had shared, the other man had been boisterous and happy, and was a good guy.

He might've made mistakes, but we all did. I liked the Kincaid I had seen, and I didn't want him to be in pain. Just like I didn't want Ronin in pain. But I didn't have the answers.

"What's going on in that mind of yours?" Ronin asked, trailing his finger across my chin again.

"Do you miss him?" I asked, my voice barely above a whisper.

Ronin let out a breath. "Yes." He sighed. "I always have. I missed what we had, more than I missed what we had as a triad with Alexis. Or maybe because Alexis broke both of us, and then Kincaid left, and I felt like I did everything wrong. That I wasn't good enough. He ghosted me."

Ronin leaned back against the couch and closed his eyes. This was my husband, the man I trusted more than anything. And he was honest with me—not something everybody had. There was no jealousy, not for the way Ronin loved and cared for those around him.

He was so open and willing to help anyone in his circle. I couldn't be jealous of how my man had loved another in his past. But I *could* ache for the fact that he didn't have what he once had.

"Now that you know, though, do you know what you feel?" I asked, cringing. "That's not a very helpful thing to ask."

Ronin sighed and rested his hand on my thigh. His thumb slid along my jeans, and I rested my head on his shoulder, needing to touch him. "I loved him, Julia. You know that. But you're my wife."

I let out a little growl. "That is not a very good thing to say."

Ronin sat up and frowned at me. "What?"

"You can't say, 'Of course, I miss him, but you're my wife,' as if I'm a barrier holding you back from your one great love." I rolled my eyes, and Ronin narrowed his. He reached out, cupped my cheek, his fingers curling around the back of my head, and pulled me closer. My breath caught, and I met his gaze.

"Don't you ever tell me—don't you ever think that I would want another more than I want you. You are mine. I'm very possessive. I might have misspoken, but don't you dare take offense at the fact that you are my wife. That means I love you. I am never giving you up. I'm never letting anything stand in our way."

I let out a shaky breath and closed my eyes. He pulled me closer, kissed me softly. And I smiled against his lips. "I love when you get all alpha and growly."

"I can't help it. You melt into a puddle of goo when I do. And I love being able to pick you up and hold you."

"That was very romantic. A little gooey, but I'll let it slide," I said on a laugh.

He kissed me hard, bit my lip, and didn't bother licking away the sting. Instead, I leaned against him and closed my eyes. "What are we going to do about Kincaid?" I asked, knowing something was bubbling beneath the surface that I needed to figure out for myself, not get from

Ronin.

Ronin paused as if he were measuring his words carefully. "I think you'd like him." Another pause. "He'd be good to have in our circle."

"He needs a friend," I agreed.

Ronin let out a soft groan. I wasn't even sure he was aware that he'd done it. "You're right. He does need…friends."

I didn't break at that little pause before the word *friends*. Because I understood it. My husband might still love Kincaid, and without the barrier of lies and betrayal, he might feel free to allow himself to do so. That meant I had to broach a subject that we might've talked about before in passing, but it wasn't easy when it was reality.

"Ronin?" I asked, my voice soft.

He leaned away from me and looked at my face. "I don't know if I like the tone of your voice. Whenever you get this way, I always feel like something's about to explode."

I punched him softly on the shoulder, and he smiled at me. I'd fallen in love with that smile on our third date. Actually, if I didn't lie to myself, I knew it was probably our first date.

"You and I have talked about possibly finding a third for us."

Ronin went impossibly still, and I wasn't even sure he was breathing.

"We love each other, but we both know that we've been talking about looking to see who we might add to make our family even…more."

"Yes, but, Julia, it's not as easy as that."

"No relationship is easy. And it isn't as if we're going to put an ad on Craigslist."

That made Ronin laugh. "I do believe there are other sites besides Craigslist."

"I don't want to use a site. I want it to happen organically, that's something we both decided. And I know that I might not have been in a triad before, but my friends have, and it's something I've always felt that I could be a part of. A polyamorous relationship has always been in my mind as my possible happily ever after. And seeing our friends have that love has reaffirmed that maybe that's something *I* could have. Or want. And I know it's the same for you. Hell, you had one before."

"And it crashed and burned," Ronin said lightly, even though the subject was anything but light.

My heart broke for him, even as it twisted at what I was saying. "I know. And I know it's complicated, but if we go in with open eyes and reaffirm who we are to each other first, maybe we can work this out."

"You're saying all the things that we've talked to each other about before—finding a possible third if the subject ever came up. But this is Kincaid, Julia." He paused. "You are talking about Kincaid, aren't you?"

I laughed. "Yes. You love him," I whispered, saying the words I needed to. Ronin shook his head, then I frowned. "We don't lie to each other, Ronin."

"I'm not lying to you. I loved the man that I was with before. I don't know this Kincaid. He's changed. So have I. It's hard to imagine opening my heart to him while also sharing you. And you would be the center of it all."

"Is that how you imagine it working out?" I asked softly.

"You are the center of *my* world. If I were to have anyone else as part of that world, you would still be the center."

My heart filled, and I blinked back tears. "I always forget that you're a former soldier turned librarian. You are so beautiful with the words."

"I am a Marine, thank you very much. Do not call me a soldier."

I laughed. "I'm sorry. Totally did it on purpose, but I am sorry. It's not like I called you an airman or something."

Ronin let out a little growl and kissed me softly. "Julia, if we try to start something with Kincaid, it could blow up in our faces and hurt everybody in the process."

"I know," I whispered. "But there's something there, Ronin. I know you felt it when we held each other."

I watched Ronin's throat work as he swallowed hard. "There might've been something, but there're so many threads that could untangle… or not… or I could ruin a horrible metaphor." His eyes danced with laughter, even though I saw the panic there, too.

"I'm not saying we get down on bended knee and ask him to marry us," I said directly.

That made my husband smile. "That might be moving a little fast, even for us."

"But maybe we can see if Kincaid wants to be our friend. And perhaps one day something more. Or, we ask him out on a date, just to see. I don't know exactly how all this works, and it's not like there's a handbook. Or if there is, it's not what we need because our lives aren't cookie-cutter and don't follow an easy checklist. But there's something there, Ronin. I love you enough to know that Kincaid was part of your past, and he might be part of your future. And it would be a disservice to both of us if we let him walk away."

I knew this was right, even though it was the hardest thing I had ever done. It likely wouldn't make sense to anyone outside of our relationship, and people might think we were crazy, but I knew this was right.

I loved my husband. And if it was the two of us for the rest of our lives, I would be the happiest woman on the face of this Earth.

But if there was a chance for us to have more?

Then I would take it. Because I loved Ronin, I loved him more than anything.

"God, I love you. You're so open and wonderful. And maybe...maybe we can try..." he whispered, and my heart sped up.

"Really?"

"Don't back out," he said drily.

"I'm not. I think Kincaid needs a friend. Or more. You know what I'm saying? I don't know. It feels like all of this is happening at the right time. I don't want to lose what we have, but I also know that we have the capability of *being*, of letting others into our lives. I want to take that chance. As long as you're by my side."

He cupped my face again and smiled softly. "If things get hard, or if you are hurt in any way, we walk away. You and me, Julia. Could be it for me, but you're right, I think we need to see what happens."

I smiled then and kissed my husband. I knew we were taking a step that no one else would likely take. I couldn't help but wonder if I was making a mistake or possibly taking the greatest chance of my life.

Chapter 4

Ronin

I bit my lip and stepped into the coffee shop. Ethan's sister-in-law, Madison, owned the place, and since she was also our friend Lincoln's cousin, it felt like a good, safe place to come and meet Kincaid. Julia had a business meeting and hadn't been able to join us, but if everything worked out, she would be part of this in every way imaginable.

I still felt like I was making one mistake after another as I tried to keep up with my feelings.

And the main one? Guilt. Not even anticipation. Because I never wanted to hurt my wife. Julia was the center of my world, just like I had told her. The idea that I could hurt her because we were trying to see if someone else could be part of our shared life haunted me.

I knew that as long as we were together, we could figure anything out. But saying the words wasn't enough. We would have to put those words into action, and that wouldn't be easy.

Madison was behind the counter, her blond and pink hair wrapped up in a bun on the top of her head. She grinned at me as I made my way to the counter. "Hi," I said, knowing I sounded a little off.

She gave me a weird look before she smiled. "Hey there. I didn't know you were off today."

"Marcus has things under control, and I took a long lunch.

Something I needed to do."

She searched my face and then went to the espresso machine. "Do you want your usual or more sugar? I feel like you might need more sugar."

That made me grin, and I nodded quickly. "I think I could use all the sugar you could possibly give me."

"You want to tell me what you're doing?" she asked, her voice casual. *Too* casual. She was worried about me, but I didn't blame her. I was acting out of character, and it was because I was worried. Scared. Freaked out. All of the above.

"Considering that anything I say to the Montgomerys gets passed around to the entire family pretty quickly since you're all a tight unit, I should tell you."

Madison frowned. "I can keep a secret. If that's what you want."

I shook my head. "No, you can tell Aaron. Keeping things from your husband probably isn't the best idea."

She smiled and looked down at her ring, a quick gesture that I wasn't even sure she knew she made. They were newlyweds, and I knew their courtship had been unusual, but she seemed happy.

I hoped I could find my happiness too. No, that wasn't right. I'd already found my happy. Now, I needed to keep it without changing it irrevocably.

"Anything you say to your barista is like talking to your bartender. Or your therapist. Maybe. I'm not a hundred percent sure because most of the time, people want coffee and they leave. But I am here for you."

I couldn't help but smile at that. "You really are."

"Of course, I am. Now, this is your usual with extra whipped cream and caramel sauce. You're going to have to brush your teeth a little extra today once you're done with it because the amount of sugar is probably not the best thing for you. But sometimes, we need that kick."

I reached into my wallet, and she shook her head. "No need to pay this time. All I need is for you to tell me what you're thinking right now."

I grimaced. "That was one way to get it out of me."

She smiled. "Ronin."

I sighed. "My ex-boyfriend is meeting me here because Julia and I have decided to ask him out on a date."

The place was nearly empty since it was an off time, and there wasn't a rush, but I still looked over my shoulder as I said that, afraid someone might hear.

I never wanted to hide who I was, but it didn't mean I needed to blast all my insecurities while still figuring out my path.

Madison, to her credit, only widened her eyes a fraction before giving me a quick nod. "Well, then. That's a lot. And it's good, right? You're happy?"

I took a moment before I nodded. "Yes, I think so. It was Julia's idea. The fact that she can't be here right now when I do this tells me that while it might have been her idea, she still wants me to be the one to say it."

"Because you might be the one who needs to," Madison whispered. "It's not easy putting yourself out there, but you're the one with the connection. And perhaps she knows that you need to be the one to speak to him first."

"You know, sometimes I think once you marry into the Montgomerys, you become wise in things. It's a little weird."

Madison shrugged. "Believe me, I know. It gets weirder the longer you're with them."

"Thankfully, we're not looking to add a Montgomery to our relationship."

"I don't know. If you're ever looking for a fourth, I hear there's a whole set of cousins that are all nice and single."

I resisted the urge to roll my eyes. "Let me make sure I don't ruin everything I already have and love by adding one person before I think about adding another." I frowned. "No. I wouldn't add a fourth. That doesn't feel right."

Madison paused. "The idea of adding one, Kincaid in particular, sounds and feels right?"

"Maybe. And that's why I'm here. And all the while, I'm promising myself I'm not going to hurt my wife."

"You won't. You're a good person, Ronin."

"I sure as hell hope so."

The hairs on the back of my neck stood on end, and Madison's smile widened. "So, is Kincaid the sexy redhead coming in with eyes only for you?"

"Behave," I whispered. Madison made a zipping motion with her fingers over her mouth, her eyes twinkling.

I took my coffee, gave her a tight nod, and braced myself as I turned.

Kincaid stood there, his jeans tight across his thighs, his T-shirt worn but not scraggly looking. His hair was out of control, curling at the ends, and he needed to trim his beard, but it still looked sexy as fuck. He had full sleeve tattoos, and from what I remembered, more tattoos down his back and sides. He was the most beautiful man I had ever seen, rugged and sexy as hell.

And he had only gotten better with age.

My heart thumped in my chest, and I hoped to hell we weren't making a mistake.

But I had missed Kincaid.

And I loved my wife.

So, if this was what Julia wanted, then maybe I should allow myself to want it, as well.

Kincaid smiled at me, but the expression didn't reach his eyes. Oh, yes, he was as confused as I was. That was good. Or weird.

Probably weird.

I tilted my head, indicating an empty table in the alcove where no one could overhear, and Kincaid gave me a tight nod. I went to the table, and Kincaid went to get himself a drink.

Madison was sweet and unassuming, and I was happy that she didn't grill him. Not that I thought she would. She was good people—all of the Montgomerys were. And I was grateful that I had them in my life. But I couldn't think about them right now. No, this was all about Kincaid. And Julia.

My touchstone and my center.

Kincaid slid into the seat across the table from me, a black coffee in his hand. The man I had once loved with all of my heart looked down at the sugary concoction in front of me and raised a brow.

"Madison and I figured I needed a little jolt."

Kincaid shook his head and sipped his coffee. "Damn, this is good."

"Madison is the best. She finds great beans and roasts them to perfection."

Kincaid looked around the place. "I like it. There's another little bakery and café around the corner, too."

"A friend of a friend owns that one. They're not in competition, though. They simply feed into each other. But yeah, good coffee all around."

"Good to know," Kincaid said softly, tapping his fingers on his mug.

"You're probably wondering why I asked you here."

"Just a little," he said tentatively.

Thank God for the sugar, I needed it. "Julia and I were talking—"

Kincaid cut in. "I like your wife. Looks like you did well. Not that, you know, it matters what I think. Just thought I should say something."

That made me smile. Maybe this would be easier than I thought. Or not. "Julia's amazing. She was the best thing that ever happened to me at that time in my life. We fit as soon as we met each other."

Kincaid smiled, this one reaching his eyes. "Hell, I'm glad you found her. Sucks for me, but then again, I'm glad you're at least talking to me and not throwing shit at me."

I shook my head and resisted the urge to reach out to him. "Anyway, Julia and I were talking about you."

Kincaid's jaw tightened. "I am sorry for bursting into your house like that. I honestly didn't know you were married. I never want to come between you and Julia. I really do like her."

I let out another breath. "I'm glad you like her. Because Julia wanted to ask you something."

"And yet, you're the one here?" Kincaid asked.

I ran my hand over my face. "Yeah...and I'm doing a shit job of it, too."

"Maybe, but why don't you tell me what you're thinking?"

"Julia and I were talking. And while she should be here, I think she put me in this situation so I would sit down face-to-face with you."

"What situation?"

"We'd like to ask you over for dinner," I said quickly, then took a sip of my sugary drink.

Kincaid blinked slowly. "Okay. I'm trying to figure out what you're saying here. Because I miss you, Ronin. And as much as I want to say that you and I can just be friends, and I can hang out with you and your wife, I don't think I'm strong enough for that."

I let out a shaky breath. "And that's why we want to ask you over for dinner...as a date."

Kincaid froze. "Run that by me again?"

"Julia and I haven't been actively looking, but we *have* talked about finding a third for our relationship. That is something we've discussed, and she's the one who brought it up now. I don't know if this is a good idea or if we're going to ruin everything we could have, but something in my gut—and something sure as hell in hers—says that maybe we can work something out. That maybe you being here right now when we're looking to perhaps add another to our relationship is important."

I watched as Kincaid ran his hands through his curls. "You're asking me out on a date. With both you and your wife."

"I know it's stupid," I mumbled.

"No, it's not. It's sort of how you and I asked Alexis out," Kincaid growled.

I flinched. "Julia isn't Alexis."

"You know, from the way that Julia looks at you, from the way she opened her arms to me when I was sitting in your house, invading everyone's space, I could tell that immediately. But, Ronin, what do you want?"

I met his gaze. "I don't know yet. But I do know that I missed you. And I love my wife, and she wants to see what happens, and that lets me think that *I* want to see what happens. We could mess this up. And we could only end up friends in the end. But Julia? She's the center of my universe. I don't want to lose that, but I don't want to lose you again either."

I was baring my soul to this man, and I felt like I was making all the mistakes, but he looked at me and then reached out and traced his finger along my palm.

And then his fingers went to the ring on my second to furthest finger and tapped the metal there.

"This isn't like dating before," Kincaid said. "You're already very much entangled."

"I am. And when you come over for dinner, you can see exactly how. But I don't know, Kincaid. I don't know what's going to happen, but this feels right."

"I'm going to be an idiot if I say yes."

"Maybe."

"But I could be even more of an idiot if I say no."

And then Kincaid pulled his hand back and gave me a tight nod. "We can see. Just dinner. And if I walk away just being your friend and Julia's? Then maybe that's okay with me. Because from what I saw from your wife, she's amazing."

"She's more than," I corrected.

"Most likely. And I don't want you to get hurt or hurt her in what we do."

"Then let's not. Let's figure it out."

"When is dinner?" the former love of my life asked, and the world fell away around me, yet it clicked into place inside me at the same time.

We might be making the gravest of mistakes, but something inside me told me we should take the leap.

I wasn't a simple man, nor were the two people that had wrapped themselves around me. And maybe that was okay. Perhaps we could work this out. Or maybe I would end up hurting the woman I loved, and the man that I thought maybe I could have again.

Chapter 5

Kincaid

Did one bring flowers or chocolates to visit their ex-boyfriend and his wife?

I didn't know the answer to that, but I still brought flowers. For both Ronin and Julia. I had no idea what I was doing, and I was pretty sure that I was going to end up hurting somebody in the process of this, but I couldn't back away. I was a masochist, a sadist, all of those things, at least when it came to my feelings for Ronin—and possibly now Julia.

I'd only met her once, and because she was so important to Ronin, she had to be important to me. Maybe tonight I would find the true woman beneath the labels, though I wasn't sure what I would do with any revelations that came up after I left.

I still wasn't sure how I had come to be here. Yet Ronin had asked, as had Julia, even if she hadn't been in the room. Only, that was a lie. She had been in the room between Ronin and me. She stood between us, but not as a barrier, as another point of connection. And now it was time to explore exactly what that meant. I rang the doorbell, trepidation sliding over my skin.

The door opened nearly as soon as I touched the button, and Julia stood on the other side, soft gray slacks covering her legs, fitted tightly around her thighs and hips. She had on a flowy blouse thing that looked complicated with all its twists around the arms and neck, but it just showcased her curves and gave the barest hint of cleavage.

It made my mouth water, and I had to tell myself it was too soon for those thoughts. We were taking the initial steps to see what could be. Me lusting after Ronin's wife wasn't the right direction to begin in, especially at full speed.

"You're here." Julia smiled. She wore heels that made her nearly tall enough to kiss my cheek. She still went up onto her tiptoes, slid her arm over my shoulder, and pressed her lips to my skin.

"I love your beard." She pulled away and smiled at me, kindness in her eyes. She put everyone at ease, and I had no idea what to do with that. Any tension I'd held earlier flowed right out of me, though I knew it would come back the instant I took a step inside. But being near her relaxed me.

It was a gift, one I hadn't truly known others could possess.

"I trimmed it a bit," I said sheepishly, my hands too full for me to rub them over my face like I wanted. "I kind of like the thing, though. The longer it gets, the more blond streaks end up mixed in with the red."

"I like it, although finding skin to kiss is very interesting." She took a step back and let me into the house. "Welcome to our home. Again."

I handed her the bouquet of wildflowers, and her eyes brightened. "These are beautiful, Kincaid. Thank you." Her gaze went to the other bouquet in my hands, and she grinned wickedly. "Oh, I like you."

I was a natural redhead and could feel my cheeks blush at that.

Great, this is going to be interesting.

Ronin came into the living room headed for the foyer at that moment, wiping his hands on a dishtowel. "Sorry it took me a bit, I'm on dish duty."

He smiled then, and I could see the tension in his shoulders, the careful look in his eyes. But then he met Julia's gaze, and his shoulders dropped a fraction as if she relieved that ache for him, as well.

What kind of gift did this woman have? It seemed I was about to find out.

"These are for you," I said, clearing my throat.

Ronin's gaze went to the flowers in my hands, then to the matching bouquet in Julia's.

He ducked his head and cleared his throat. "You know, I don't think I've ever received flowers before." He reached out, and I gave him the bouquet, our fingers brushing. A shock sizzled between us, and I swallowed hard, telling myself that I could not take a step back. If I did, I'd hurt Ronin, and I'd already done enough of that.

"I can't believe I haven't," Julia said, tapping her lip. "I feel like I've been remiss. You just wait. You're going to get surprise flowers now." She leaned in and kissed her husband before taking the bouquet from him. "I have matching vases that will work perfectly for the dinner table."

"Get comfortable, Kincaid. We have a sparkling cider and a few nonalcoholic drinks that we made for you."

I shook my head. "I'm good with water."

She raised a brow. "You're welcome to have anything you'd like. Tonight will be a dry evening."

I frowned. "You don't have to refrain because I'm here. I'm fine with people drinking around me."

Ronin interrupted. "And I'm glad to hear it. If we do this again, or whenever we meet again, we might have that drink. But tonight, Julia and I decided that it'd be good to have clear heads." Our eyes met. "Or at least as clear as they can be in this case."

I swallowed hard. "Then sparkling cider sounds good."

"I can mix it with a peach puree if you're interested," Julia said, her voice echoing out from the kitchen area.

"I'd try it. She's a whiz at that. Some of our friends own cafes like that one we met in. And they've been having fun coming up with different drinks so they can make them at home."

"Oh, that sounds good." I raised my voice. "I'll take one of those."

"Me too, babe," Ronin called out, our gazes never leaving each other.

My dick had already hardened, and not just for the man in front of me. Okay, then, this was going to be an interesting evening.

"I like your home," I said, and let out a shaky laugh. "I think I said that the first time I was here."

"It's a good home. It's one story, as you can see from the outside." I looked down as Ronin tapped his thigh. "Easier for me."

"And let's be honest, me too," Julia said, her hands full. I beat Ronin to her and took two glasses from her hands.

I met her gaze. "I could have helped. I didn't know you were making them right away."

"It's okay. I waitressed for a while in high school and college. I'm pretty good at it."

"And yet, you were just about to say something about how you trip up stairs, and that's why we like a one-story house?" Ronin asked, laughter in his tone.

She stuck her tongue out at him. "Oh, shush. I'm usually better at glassware. Marginally." She paused. "Okay. From now on, I will ask for help."

"Good girl," Ronin said, and my dick hardened even more at the heated gaze they exchanged.

Julia held up her glass, and I did the same, Ronin at my side between us. "To tonight. New beginnings."

"And learning to relax," Julia added, and I met her gaze, then Ronin's, and clinked our glasses together. Each of the glasses met as one, the ringing sound loud in my ears.

I let out a breath and then put the glass to my mouth. I took a sip, and then I let out a groan of surprise. "This is awesome."

Julia beamed. "Yay. I made a bunch, and I have other things I can try. Ronin and I honestly don't drink that much."

"We've been looking for different ways to get flavor without constantly just mixing orange juice into things," Ronin said, shaking his head.

"If it's anything like these, count me in," I said, not realizing I had said the words until they were out of my mouth.

Those words spoke of promise, futures, and I didn't know where we were now, let alone where we'd be later.

"I'm going to break the ice and ask what exactly I'm doing here tonight," I said suddenly, needing to get the words out.

Ronin scowled, but Julia smiled. "Oh, good. I don't have a to-do or checklist, but that was first on my options before we sat down for a meal."

"And that would be my wife," Ronin said, grinning. "I may be the librarian, but she is the computational chemist and data analyst. She takes order and research even more seriously than I do."

I shook my head. "I'm only slightly organized when it comes to work. Not so much when it comes to everything else."

"I remember," Ronin added. Again, those memories slid between us, but at least they weren't so overwhelming that I couldn't breathe.

"I'll whip you into shape," Julia said, giving me a small nod like a little drill sergeant.

"Okay, you can try." I shook my head.

"Oh, I think I'll enjoy it."

Was this flirting? It was a date, wasn't it?

"As for why you're here," Ronin began, and my attention drifted to him, the tension I felt earlier coming right back. "We're on a date, and while I would like for us to be out in public with our first date, I figured with the many undercurrents that are no doubt here, it'd be better for us not to have to deal with the public's reaction to seeing a, *gasp*, triad in the wild."

Julia rolled her eyes. "We have two triads in our lives already that are now married and either working on babies or already have them. They are amazing but still have to deal with people being stupid out in the real world."

I met Ronin's gaze for an instant before I looked back at Julia. "I remember that feeling. Not the babies and things, but the looks. And that was a few years ago. People seem to have gotten a little bit better over time."

Julia shook her head. "A lot of people *are* more accepting, but others seem to take that acceptance as a way for them to feel more comfortable making things that aren't their business the center of their lives. Their intolerance and prejudice becomes more flagrant the freer the people who aren't like them find themselves. Our friends deal with it, and if we want to do this again or if we decide that the three of us together out in public is what we want, we will have to deal with the fact that not everyone will be happy with this relationship. But I had to deal with the same thing when I was dating a woman, and I know you guys have had to deal with some other things while you were dating each other and when Alexis was involved."

I shook my head, blinking and trying to keep up. "You really put it all out there, don't you?" I asked.

Julia shrugged and took another sip of her drink. "If I didn't, we'd be dancing around it for the rest of the evening and probably keeping up with secrets and lies or hurt feelings. If we don't say it, then we'll end up hurting one another, and I don't want that."

She took another big gulp. I had a feeling she wished there was real champagne in that glass rather than sparkling cider.

"Are you okay, honey?" Ronin asked, cupping her face. Julia nodded and smiled softly at her husband.

The longing from before stabbed me, but I pushed it back. They'd been married for years now. Knew each other in ways that I hadn't even known Ronin. And while I might be jealous, it wasn't because I wasn't part of it, it was because I wanted what they had, as well.

"I guess if you're going to be that open and honest, I should be, too," I said after a beat, not knowing if interrupting their intimate moment was the right thing to do but knowing that I probably should. If they wanted me here, then I couldn't hide.

"What is it that you want?" Julia asked, as Ronin stared at me. Julia might be the one speaking the most tonight, but I knew Ronin's thoughts were running at full speed. If he had something to say, he would. Until then, Julia would speak for both of them as if they had talked for hours about what they needed to say.

Once again, I wasn't jealous, but I wanted it.

"I'm going to be honest and tell you that I came here for Ronin," I said quickly, and the light in Julia's eyes dimmed for the barest moment. "Shit, I meant before this date, when I first came to town. Not tonight."

The tension in Ronin's jaw eased, and I barely noticed it at first, I was so focused on the idea that I had hurt Julia.

"I mean it. I came here to try and fix things with Ronin, only I didn't know that he was already married. And if you two hadn't decided to ask me here tonight, I never would have stepped in like this. I might have found a way to eventually become friends with both of you—once I got over myself—but I wouldn't have broached the subject." I sucked in a breath. "Not because it isn't appealing to me—because fuck yes, it is— but because it wouldn't have been my place."

"So, what do you want out of tonight?" Ronin asked.

"Maybe the same as you? Just wondering what the possibilities are. I don't want to give full promises of forever because it's a single night, one date, and doing so would harm all of us. But I think there's something here. Enough that maybe we should see."

"That's our thinking, too," Julia said. She laughed. "Anyone outside listening to this conversation would probably wonder what the hell we are talking about. I know it's not what some people think is normal, and I'm fine with that. But I love that we're all trying to be so open and honest, even though I know it isn't easy."

"How about we sit for dinner and talk about where you've been, and what we've been doing? We don't need to go into full declarations and promises tonight."

I looked at Ronin. "That works for me. However, I *will* make one promise," I said, and Julia laughed while Ronin rolled his eyes.

"Of course, you have to be the one who gets the last word," Ronin grumbled.

"That was me, and possibly still is me. I want to learn the Ronin you are now and get to know the woman that he fell in love with. And if we're being honest, yes, I'm attracted to both of you," I said quickly.

Julia blushed, and Ronin snorted. "Yes, that sounds like the Kincaid I knew."

That sobered me a bit, but not entirely. "I'm not that Kincaid anymore, but I am blunt enough. You're both fucking hot, and that's not going to change. I say what's on my mind, and yes, that's gotten me into trouble more than once."

"I remember," Ronin said, the look in his eyes heated.

"Now you're going to have to tell me the story," Julia said, and then she held out her hand.

I looked at it for a moment and then slid my hand into hers. She gave it a squeeze, and then Ronin was on her other side, his hand on the small of her back.

"Let's go get something to eat."

I followed them, wondering how the hell this was my life, but knowing that maybe I needed to take this chance.

Chapter 6

Julia

I smiled into my glass, doing my best not to laugh and shoot water out of my nose. That'd nearly happened twice already, and I had a feeling if I wasn't careful, Kincaid and Ronin were going to send me right over the edge.

Over what, though? Perhaps not only laughter. No, I had a feeling it had to do with the way they looked at each other and then at me. There were different kinds of tension bubbling beneath the surface. And it didn't only have to do with the past these two men in front of me shared. It had more to do with what could happen *after* dinner.

The idea that I could want someone in such a similar way to how I wanted Ronin might have shamed me if I had been in another place in my life. But I had grown into the woman I was. I was sure of myself. I'd had to be after walking away from my parents and trying to find my own way. They hadn't supported me, and I had lost their love long ago, but I had found the woman I needed to become. And that woman loved her husband, *craved* him. But she also wanted the man currently giving sex eyes to her spouse.

I took another sip of my water, my mouth parched. Apparently, my mind was going in a very dirty direction, even if I had told myself that might not happen tonight.

Only I saw the longing glances, and not merely between them. No, it was between the *three* of us. And I wasn't sure we would be able to hold back much longer, not with the way we all looked at one another.

"And can you believe that the one day I was trying to get an actual portrait of this man, he kept flipping me off the entire time? All he had to do was act like his serious and brooding self. Instead, he couldn't stop smiling." Kincaid laughed, and I grinned.

"Ronin smiles. He's not all serious and broody." I looked over at my husband, who shrugged.

"Sometimes, I can't even hold back laughter." He did his best to keep a very stern expression on his face, and then grinned, his mouth twitching. "Okay, fine. I suck at acting seriously when I'm supposed to be. I'm not very good at it. I only brood when others think I shouldn't."

I shook my head and leaned into Ronin's side. We were sitting on the couch, relaxing after a delicious dinner of roasted chicken stuffed with lemon and garlic and served with mashed potatoes and steamed carrots. I had made cookies that morning, needing to keep my hands busy, and a few of them were still left on the table.

Kincaid sat on the other side of the couch, and while I was close to him, we weren't touching. Ronin sat facing the front, although his head was turned to us, my back to Ronin's side, my feet tucked up under me as my body was positioned towards Kincaid. He had his back against the corner of the couch, one knee up, so the three of us were looking at one another, all nearly touching, or in my case with my husband, touching just enough.

I couldn't be the only one sensing the rising heat in the air. But I had been the one to broach the subject so much already. Should I be the one to do so again?

"You should tell him about the time you entered that wet T-shirt contest," Ronin whispered, his voice deep against my ear.

I knew he had done it on purpose, that low growl sending shivers right to my nipples. They pebbled, my whole body growing tight. I pressed my thighs together and looked up at Kincaid's eyes. The light blue darkened ever so slightly, his cheeks turning red. But that wasn't embarrassment.

No, that was all me.

"Wet T-shirt contest?" His gaze deliberately moved to my breasts. They were not small. In fact, they felt even more substantial than usual. I was all curves, much to my mother's displeasure. Not that I had ever cared what she thought of me. I filled out my shirts, and now the lace of my bra scraped against my nipples every time I took a breath. It was hard for me to breathe just then with the tension in the air.

I swallowed hard, licking my suddenly dry lips. Ronin gently brushed his knuckles down the skin of my arm, and I sucked in another breath, trying to calm myself.

I cleared my throat. "The guy I was dating at the time didn't believe I'd do it."

"I was in the audience," Ronin said, his voice still deep, sending shivers down my back. I pressed my thighs together again, my clit pulsing, just from the look in Kincaid's eyes, and Ronin's heated body pressed against my back. "I didn't know it was her at the time. We met for real later, over that book."

"And did you win?"

I grinned, moving my shoulders back in pride, the action pressing my breasts into the front of my shirt more. "Of course, I did. And I never saw that little fucker again. He was rude about it," I added as Kincaid frowned, his gaze moving between my eyes and my chest. "He thought I didn't have the gumption to go up and take off my bra and do a wet T-shirt contest with the rest of the girls. And then when I dared to do it, he got all caveman and tried to tug me out of there."

Ronin growled. "I remember another person coming in and punching the shit out of him."

"You?" Kincaid asked, looking over my head at Ronin.

I felt Ronin shake his head. "Another guy. A friend of hers from college."

"Just a friend. And I did not like the way my ex got grabby, so that was the last of him. Either way, though, I won. My breasts were amazing."

"Were?" Ronin chuckled, his voice rough. His hands slid down my arm, just a brush, a touch, and I sucked in a sharp breath, my entire body vibrating. Once again, I pressed my legs together, needing the friction. He reached out and gripped my knee, spreading my legs slightly. Not so much that Kincaid could see anything—after all, I was wearing pants—but enough to give Ronin control.

"Not yet," he whispered and bit my earlobe.

I moaned, forcing my eyes open as I looked at Kincaid.

He shifted in his seat, and my gaze traveled down his body, landing on his very rock-hard erection, straining against his jeans. Given the length of him behind his zipper, I knew that if we did this, it would hurt in the best way possible.

"I was going to ask if you needed coffee or anything," Ronin whispered, his attention on Kincaid and me. "But I don't know if I need the extra caffeine."

I let out a small laugh, the sound tangling with Kincaid's rough chuckle.

"I can leave right now, and you guys can finish your evening," Kincaid said, setting his glass down on the table.

I frowned, wondering if I had misread the situation.

Ronin kissed my temple before slowly running his hand down my thigh. My legs spread of their own accord, and I blushed, trying to press them together again, but then Ronin pushed back.

"You don't need to leave. You can do whatever you'd like, but I do believe we need ground rules."

"Ground rules?" Kincaid repeated slowly.

I cleared my throat, knowing it was my turn to speak. "Yes, you know me and rules. They are my favorite." My voice sounded breathless, heady with anticipation. I didn't even sound like myself.

I loved it.

"Ronin is my husband, and I love him, and tonight I want to make love with him. And I would love it if you joined us." My cheeks heated, and I wondered how the hell I'd ended up here.

Ronin laughed behind me and kissed me again. "Julia and I talked before you came. We are both in agreement that whatever happens tonight does not need to be permanent. But we *do* need to make sure we discuss what happens. If we want this to happen again, or if this is just to be one night."

Kincaid looked at us, and was silent for so long that I was afraid I had made a mistake. Still, I did not press my legs together.

"I don't know if, after today, I can walk away," Kincaid said, and relief poured through me.

I didn't know him, but I wanted to.

"We'll take this as it comes," Ronin said. "Just the three of us."

"Just the three of us." Kincaid looked at us and nodded. "No, I don't think a fourth in any fashion is what is needed. Or what any of us wants. I'm not Alexis."

Ronin stiffened behind me. "I don't think any of us are."

I needed to speak. "Good, because this is getting serious, and I'm kind of freaking out. So if someone could kiss me, that'd be great."

Ronin bit my earlobe, and I moaned, but it was Kincaid who moved forward. He cupped my face, his hands reaching around and tugging on my hair slightly. The bit of pain urged me on, and I groaned, leaning forward. He looked at me, his eyes stark with need, and then he crushed his mouth to mine.

I moaned, arcing for him, but doing so pressed me closer to Ronin from behind. My husband's hands slid up my shirt and cupped my breasts, plucking at my nipples through the lace. It was the exact kind of pain and heady sensations I needed—a man who knew my body in every way possible.

"You taste sweet," Kincaid growled against me.

"You should taste her everywhere," Ronin whispered.

I blushed, my hand rising. Kincaid sighed. He froze. "I'd like that. If you give me permission."

I looked at him and then nodded. Then I arched my neck slightly so I could look at Ronin. "Just the three of us. For tonight. While we figure this out."

"Anything you want, Julia. I love you."

He kissed me softly, and I sank into him. "I love you, too."

"Now, let's have fun with this."

Ronin cleared his throat. "Let's go to the bedroom first, though. Only because this angle might not be great for my leg."

Kincaid cursed and immediately jumped up. "Shit, I forgot."

My husband smiled. "It's okay. It means we get to have a little more fun with positions.

"Good, because I'm going to want to touch you, too," Kincaid said, then I finally pressed my thighs together as we all made our way to the bedroom. We turned the corner in the hallway, and then Kincaid lifted me up, twisting me in his arms so I wrapped my legs around his waist.

I let out a sharp gasp and looked down at him. "Really?" I asked with a laugh.

"I'm just saying, why not?"

I kissed him again and then reached out to tangle my fingers with Ronin's as we made our way to the bedroom. We had a large California King, one that I had liked because of the way Ronin and I could roll around, but I was thrilled for the extra space now.

Kincaid rested me on the edge, and then Ronin was there, standing between my legs, slowly playing with the seam of my pants.

"You ready for this, wife?" he inquired, claiming me in front of

Kincaid.

"Always," I said. "I trust you."

A visible shudder slid over my husband before he turned and looked at Kincaid.

"Please?" I asked, knowing that perhaps they needed that slight push.

And then the man that I loved and the man I already felt connected to leaned forward, and their lips brushed. That single touch was all it took. The two of them pulled one another, their mouths hungry, kisses fierce. I slowly slid my hand into my pants and over myself, touching my clit. I was already so wet, so hot. If I weren't careful, I would come right then.

Ronin pulled away, his breath coming in pants as he tugged on Kincaid's hair and then looked over at me. "I do believe our Julia is already getting started without us."

"You two have fun. I'm good right here."

Kincaid shook his head and went down to his knees in front of me. "Oh no, I do believe you need to be the center of attention for now."

And then he tugged at my pants. Ronin moved to the side of the bed, and I helped him take off my shirt, his hands slowly cupping my breasts as Kincaid worked my pants. They were both touching me, using their mouths and fingers. I could barely keep up. And then I was naked in front of them, both of them still clothed, and my legs were spread. Suddenly, Kincaid's mouth was on me.

I shifted, groaning, my fingers tangling in the sheets as I pressed into him. Ronin's mouth was on my breasts, sucking and tugging at my nipples as Kincaid lapped at me like a starving man. He spread my thighs and then pulled me to the edge of the bed, moving my legs so that my knees were practically at my shoulders. I moved with him, and he ate at me, sucking and licking until the sensation of both men's hands on me sent me over the edge.

I could barely breathe, my whole body was shaking, and when Ronin stripped off his shirt, my hands immediately moved to his flesh.

"You do taste sweet," Kincaid whispered against my pussy before he leaned back and undid his shirt.

Ronin stood up and slowly started stripping the rest of the way, while Kincaid did the same. "I'm going to need to be the one who lays down," Ronin said. "At least, tonight."

"We can do that," Kincaid said before he kissed me again.

Ronin and I had been together for years, and we knew what positions worked for us. We were creative, and from the dark glint in Kincaid's eyes, so was he.

I crawled up my husband's body, pumping his dick twice before I straddled him, kissing him hard. Kincaid came up behind me, and I looked over at him, the thick lines of him so damn sexy, I almost came again just sitting on my husband's chest. While Ronin was a bit slenderer, his dick was thicker than Kincaid's, but Kincaid was longer.

The fact that I was sitting here comparing dick sizes and loving that I would be able to play with both of them made everything suddenly seem far too real.

"What are you up for tonight?" Kincaid asked, looking at both of us.

He slowly slid his hand over my back and played between my cheeks. I leaned into him and groaned.

"We can do that," I whispered. "I think the idea of both of you inside me at the same time might kill me, but in the best ways."

"There's lube and condoms in the drawer," Ronin said, lifting his chin. "We play often enough that she should be ready. You still need to be careful."

"Always," Kincaid promised, his gaze intense. And then he leaned over and kissed me, and I could taste myself on him. I groaned, needing more, but then he pulled away. Ronin tapped on my thigh, and I grinned at him. "Saddle up," he whispered, and I crawled up his body and held onto the headboard. He spread my thighs and laughed at me, and I groaned, rocking on his face as he sent me into orgasm. My body shaking, my breasts heavy, I leaned back, grateful that Kincaid was somehow there, his hand on my breast, the other playing between my cheeks. He worked me, played with me, and when he started fucking me with his fingers, I arched, needing more.

But then he pulled me away, just enough that I could see his face.

"First, before I take you there," he said, pressing firmly against me, "let's suck your husband's dick," he whispered, winking.

I laughed, loving that I could in this moment. I crawled over Ronin, kissing Kincaid, and then my husband, and then both Kincaid and I made our way to the glory that was my husband's cock. I laughed inwardly at that thought before looking up the length of him. Kincaid did the same, and we met at the tip, kissing before going back. I lapped at Ronin's balls while Kincaid swallowed Ronin whole, hollowing his cheeks and going deep. We both hummed against him, and Ronin cursed, tugging at my hair. "I am not going to come right now. I want to be in your pussy when I do."

I pulled away, and Kincaid tapped at my hip. "Why don't you ride him, and then I'll ride you."

I shivered, but then I bent over and pumped Kincaid's dick, loving the way he groaned. I saw the scars on his body, which I knew he likely wouldn't want to talk about right now, but we would. I loved his ink, but I wanted to know all about him. I was giving my body to him and my husband. I hoped he would give us something more.

I pushed those thoughts out of my mind, knowing we just needed to focus on what we were doing. I swallowed Kincaid, needing his taste, as both Ronin and Kincaid had their hands on me, playing with my breasts, my pussy. And then I pulled away, reacting when Kincaid shoved hard, and I groaned, my mouth on his.

And then I straddled my husband and sank onto his cock. I groaned, my body stretching to accommodate him. As I leaned forward, kissing him, Ronin reached around, spreading my cheeks for Kincaid, and I felt the coolness of the lube before Kincaid started working me again.

"Ready?" Kincaid asked, his voice rough as he licked up my spine and latched on to my neck. I moaned, my whole body shaking as I rode Ronin. My husband had his hands on me, his mouth on me, and when Kincaid reached over my shoulder to kiss the love of my life, I almost came right there, but I forced myself back, knowing if I did, I would miss it all.

"Please," I begged.

And then Kincaid slowly worked himself inside me. I was so full, it was nearly too much, yet just enough. I needed the pain, the pleasure even more so.

And when Kincaid was fully seated, the same as Ronin, they each took a breast, met each other's gazes, and moved. I looked over my shoulder at Kincaid, and then down at Ronin.

"Wow," I whispered, but I thought it was possibly only in my head.

When the two of them moved, the three of us arcing into one another like we'd been doing it for eons rather than just this one time, I felt like something shifted. It wasn't just Ronin and me anymore. No, this was the possibility of a future.

I knew this man in front of me, knew him with every ounce of my soul.

And I knew that he loved the man behind me, the one taking me over the edge into bliss. And it wasn't only Ronin who wanted him. There was something there, something that I craved, as well. I wouldn't have let him touch me otherwise.

And when the three of us came, I could barely keep my thoughts together. But I knew that we would have to talk once I did. We would have to take a breath.

Because I could not have this only be the past. I couldn't have this be something that broke us. It was a promise of something bigger than any of us, even though the complications could implode and hurt us all in the end. I needed this. Needed to see what was next even with the thought that we could lose it all.

I was utterly terrified that if we weren't careful, this could be the last time. The only time.

Chapter 7

Julia

It was two weeks after our date with Kincaid, and while I might not be sore anymore, I swore I could still feel them on either side of me, holding me close as we came together. The three of us hadn't been together since that night, though we'd gone on several smaller dates and dinners. I was glad that we had given each other space and time to fall into what we were becoming, whatever that may be.

We often met at Madison's for coffee since it was a safe space, as well as another café owned by a friend of ours. We'd had dinner at our house once more, but it hadn't led to anything but a goodnight kiss and a promise of what was to come. We might've started out with the proverbial bang, but we were taking it slowly now. And I was grateful. Every night, I turned into my husband's arms, and we made love. We held each other. And I couldn't help but wonder what Kincaid was doing. When I voiced that to Ronin, he had said much the same.

I knew if we continued down this path, Ronin and Kincaid would soon go out together without me, and I didn't feel even a single twinge of jealousy at that. It was what a true triad was, even if we weren't thinking of permanence but rather connection right now. One day, I might go out with Kincaid on my own, and I was grateful for that. I wanted to know the man with the sadness in his eyes and discover how he could be direct one minute and hidden the next. And I wanted Ronin to be able to find that, as well.

It was such an interesting connection, the way we all worked together, and I was grateful that I had found the other part of my soul that understood—someone who wanted the same things. However, I knew the two of them had far more to talk about than Kincaid and I might. And I didn't mind that. Because it meant that Ronin would be opening up about something that he might not fully open up to me about because I hadn't been there. And I didn't feel like I needed to pry that out of him.

I shook my head and looked down at my phone, wondering once again why I was letting my thoughts go down this path instead of getting out of the car and walking into my parents' home. I didn't want to be here today. I didn't want to be here most days. But I was a good daughter, even if no one had given me that title and never would.

But I would do what had to be done. I would talk with my parents, and then I would go home, cry, and pretend that nothing had happened.

Just like every year on this day.

My phone buzzed, and I looked down to see a text from Ronin.

Ronin: *I can still be there. Say the word, and I will leave work.*

I closed my eyes and pushed down everything that might hurt. I couldn't let the people in the house see these emotions—or *any*. They would only pounce on the opportunity.

Me: *No, I can do this. I won't be long. You need your vacation days.*

I could practically hear Ronin cursing, and I knew that Marcus would've covered for him, but I hadn't needed that. When he got off work, I would lean on him. But for now, I needed to stand on my own two feet.

I hadn't needed to go into work today because I had worked remotely over the weekend and had gotten my hours in that way. My boss was pretty amazing, and I could work from home most days as long as I had network access to the server. I liked going in and working with Ethan and the others, though. And sometimes I needed the space. But I had known that I needed today, so my boss had let everything work out the way it did.

Ronin: *I love you. Call me when you can.*

I choked back a sob, annoyed with myself for getting emotional already. I hadn't even walked through the doors yet.

Me: *I love you. And I will.*

I turned off my phone, knowing that it would only annoy my parents if it rang or buzzed, and I didn't want to add anything else to the fire.

I checked my reflection and smoothed my hair currently pulled back in a chignon at the base of my neck. My eyes were done up in subtle makeup, just enough to make them pop but not to look slutty—at least in my mother's opinion. I looked normal, like I wasn't dying inside.

As if I'd missed the fact that my sister was no longer here.

My baby sister would've had a birthday today.

She had died when she was only sixteen years old, and every day on the date of her birth, the family she left behind met. Though we didn't celebrate. Sitting around a table and watching my mother come to hate me more and more, and my father turn in on himself with each passing moment, couldn't be counted as a celebration. I was eighteen when my sister finally passed. Sixteen years old and dying of terminal liver cancer shouldn't have even been an option. Kids did not get that cancer. It was something the doctors told us repeatedly, the refrain echoing often in my ears.

But she had died, and we had broken as a family. Or perhaps we had broken long before that. My mother had pushed me away, her precious baby dying in front of her. And I never once blamed Mother for that. Never once blamed the fact that she hadn't wanted to look at me because I looked so much like Taylor. That I hadn't been there when it counted.

Taylor had been a light. Had brought so much joy. She had faced the cancer head-on and told the world that she would make something of herself. And she had, even in the few short months that we'd had her with us after the diagnosis. She didn't go to school. Instead, she worked full-time for a charity organization, donating what energy she had to helping others. My mother had been right there with her for every doctor's appointment, every moment of horror and unending unknowns.

In the end, the cancer had taken Taylor swiftly, the pain and agony no longer digging their claws into her. I missed my sister with every breath I took, with every moment I was still here. I hated that Ronin had never gotten to meet her. I even hated that Kincaid could never meet her.

She hadn't grown into the wonderful woman she could have been. I let out a shuddering breath and then got out of the car. I didn't need to wallow in the what-could-have-beens and what-had-beens. Not when I needed to face my parents.

I knocked on the door since I no longer had a key. And even if I'd had one for emergencies, they never would have let me walk right in.

Ronin could walk into his parents' home and be welcomed with open arms. He could go straight for the fridge, grab something to eat, and laugh with his mom as she rolled her eyes, patted his head, and made him a sandwich because she could. She might still work forty-hour weeks and be connected to the military even after she'd retired from active duty, but she loved her baby boy.

Honestly, I wasn't even sure the welcome mat that lay in front of my parents' door symbolized acceptance for me. My father opened the door, his face gray, the lines of the years digging grooves into his skin. He had aged during Taylor's sickness and had turned into an old man when Taylor died.

He didn't say anything, just gave me a slight nod and stepped back. I held a single lily, my baby sister's favorite flower, and walked into the room. I set the lily on the foyer table where Taylor's pictures were, a single candle lit for her, and closed my eyes tightly, doing my best to breathe.

My father didn't offer to take my bag, didn't move to help me with anything. Instead, he shuffled away, much like he had done through life.

My mother was in the living room, her head held high, a handkerchief in her hand. She looked over at me, her gaze going from my head to my toes. She gave me a slight, tight nod. "You're late."

"I'm sorry, I was in the car, and it took me a moment to get in. It's a tough day." I held back a wince, knowing I shouldn't even bring it up, even though it was the only reason I was here. Other families might discuss it, but we wouldn't. We couldn't.

My mother glanced at me and then looked straight ahead to where our family photo was, the last one we had taken. There hadn't been any more pictures on the walls after Taylor died. Not in the more than fifteen years we had lived without my sister. It was as if this house and everything in it had stopped at that moment. There had been no growth, no more living.

And I didn't know how to make it end. I didn't know how to make it better.

"I didn't cook," my mother said.

I nodded.

We had stopped having family dinners on Taylor's birthday. Instead, I came over, sat with them for a moment while we tried to rekindle something between us, and then I went home, where I'd cry and heal.

I knew this wasn't what Taylor would want, but I didn't know how to fix it. And, honestly, I didn't know if I was strong enough to continue trying.

"I'll be working on the garden soon, that's what Taylor would have wanted," my mother spoke up, and I nodded. I had been wrong. One part of the house did continue to change.

The garden in the back.

That was what my mother and Taylor had worked on day in and day out together, something just for the two of them. I had loved to garden with them, but when Taylor got sick, it'd become something for mother and daughter, and I had understood. I had backed away, and now, my mother gardened with fervor, trying to bring life into each plant as if she could bring life back into Taylor.

I hated that I couldn't do anything about that, so I only nodded tightly, knowing that soon there would be new blooms, a thrilling masterpiece of a garden that I would likely never walk into.

I wasn't welcome.

I stood in the living room as my father came back and sat down in his recliner, rocking back and forth. The creak of the old wood echoed in my ears, and I looked around, peering into the time capsule that was over fifteen years ago.

Taylor wasn't here anymore. She had long since passed on, but the shrine to her memory echoed within these walls, begging for freedom.

That was what she had wanted. Freedom. The ability to make her own choices and keep our family whole. But it hadn't worked. Taylor had found her freedom, at least I hoped—freedom from pain and from the lack of dignity that came from cancer. But our family was never the same.

And I couldn't change that.

I stood there for another twenty minutes without saying a word before I left, not bothering to look at them. They weren't looking at me.

I got into the car, leaned my head against the steering wheel, and let out a shaky breath.

"Happy birthday, Taylor," I whispered.

Then I started the car and headed towards home.

I didn't even realize I'd stopped in front of Madison's coffee shop until I was already there. I needed caffeine. Something. I didn't want to go home alone, even though I knew Ronin would be there the moment I asked him to come. I didn't want to ask him for help. He had work to do, and we had both known that today would be hard. I shouldn't need help with every single little thing.

I sighed, annoyed with myself, and went in for coffee. Madison wasn't up front, but one of her friendly staff members was. I smiled and ordered myself a chai latte, the one that came in the big mugs that usually made me happy to look at. Once in hand, I went back to one of the tables, holding back tears. I probably shouldn't be out in public, but I really didn't want to be home.

I faced the door, just needing the light, and then I looked up and suddenly realized I wasn't alone.

Kincaid stood near the table, his head tilted to the side as he studied me, a cup of coffee in a recyclable cup in his hand.

"Julia? What's wrong?"

I looked up at him and then blinked, before bursting into tears. Gut-wrenching sobs that scared even me.

Kincaid cursed, set down his coffee, and sat in the booth, somehow bringing me into his lap. Others were looking, but he waved them off, running his hands over my hair.

"Ronin said today was about your sister," he whispered, and I nodded, embarrassed that I couldn't stop crying.

Instead, Kincaid kissed the top of my head and pulled out of the booth, using his strength to carry me.

"I'm fine, don't carry me. This is embarrassing. I need to come back in here one day without having everyone remember me like this."

"They're fine. They understand."

From the way he growled it, I was pretty sure if they didn't, he'd beat them into it. It didn't matter. I didn't look at anyone. Instead, I leaned into Kincaid, needing to breathe.

"My car," I whispered.

"Oh, you're not driving, we'll come and get your car later."

"Give me the keys," Madison said, and I sniffed, looking over my shoulder.

"I'm so sorry."

"No, don't be sorry. We all need to cry sometimes. Kincaid will get you home," she said softly, giving me a searching look. "I'll get Aaron to drive your car back later. We've got you. Don't worry." She kissed my cheek, took my car keys from my purse as I tried to fumble with them, and we left after taking my house key.

Kincaid got me into the car and silently drove to my home. I wondered how the hell I'd gotten into this situation.

"I'm fine. Really."

"I already texted Ronin. He's in a meeting but will get out as soon as he can."

"He doesn't need to. I had a tough moment. I'm fine."

Kincaid glared at me, his red hair fiery in the sunlight. "I'm getting you inside, then I'm going to tuck you in, and you're going to deal with me learning this whole caring shit."

I snorted. "Oh?" I laughed. I didn't think I could laugh today. Who knew someone other than Ronin could do that for me?

"Come on. Text Ronin so he knows you're okay. At least as okay as you can be."

I pulled out my phone and leaned into Kincaid as he walked me into the house.

Me: *I'm home.*

Ronin: *Are you okay?*

Me: *I am. Kincaid's here. I feel like such an idiot.*

Ronin: *Don't. Let him take care of you. Let him hold you.*

I frowned.

Me: *What do you mean?*

Ronin: *Just let him hold you. Do what you need to do. I'll be home later. I love you.*

Me: *I love you too.*

I put my phone down and looked up as Kincaid walked into the living room, a cup of tea in his hand.

"I have no idea how to make a chai latte thingy, but you had tea and a teapot." Kincaid sat next to me and kissed me hard on the mouth, shocking me. "Did that kiss help you get out of your funk?"

I snorted, shaking my head. "I wouldn't call it a funk. I just…today sucked."

I explained in detail about my parents and my sister, and Kincaid shook his head, growling when I got to the harder parts.

"You know I want to say that I can't believe your parents would do that, but as my parents are pretty similar, I can't say that."

I set the now-cooling tea aside and looked at him. "Your parents blame you for your sister?" I whispered.

"They do. They're pretty shitty people, but I can't blame them for hating me. I hated myself for a long time. I'm only now realizing that I don't have to hate myself every day."

I reached up and cupped his face, his beard soft on my skin. "You don't need to blame yourself at all. Accidents happen."

"And you don't need to feel guilty that you are here and Taylor isn't."

I closed my eyes tightly, let out a breath, and leaned into him. "For someone who says he's not good at this whole caring thing, you sure know exactly what to say."

"Sometimes, I do. Other times I feel like I'm forty steps behind. But I'm catching up."

I looked at him, and he tucked my hair behind my ear.

"Is Ronin going to be home soon?" he asked, his voice deep.

I swallowed hard, looking at his face, my lips going dry. "He'll be home later. He told me I need to let you take care of me."

Kincaid studied my face, then tilted his head. "What do you think he meant by that?"

I let out a shaky laugh. "Knowing my husband, it could mean anything. You know Ronin."

"You know, I do. I thought maybe he had changed over the years, but he's still a man who puts everyone else before him."

"That's what he says about you," I whispered.

Kincaid snorted. "And you know what? That's what he says about you. The three of us together really need to learn to take rather than just give, right?"

"Or maybe it all balances out."

We were both silent for a moment before Kincaid leaned closer and gently brushed his lips against mine. "Can I keep kissing you?"

I wanted to feel. I wanted to *be*. In this moment with Kincaid? It felt right. It felt like what Ronin would want and what *I* wanted. And so, I leaned into him and kissed him. "Please." He kissed me back.

He ran his hands through my hair, pulling it out of its chignon, and I grinned. I hated the damn thing. He yanked me against him, and I landed on his lap, straddling him. He kept kissing, tugging my head to the side so he could lick at my neck. I rocked against him, his cock pressing against his pants.

"You're killing me."

"I want you," I whispered.

"Are you okay wanting me without Ronin here?"

I nodded. "We already talked about it. All three of us. We're duos and a trio. Ronin knows what we're doing."

Kincaid smiled. "Yes, he knows what we're doing." And then he kissed me again.

He methodically pulled up my shirt, exposing my breasts. He lowered the lacy cups of my bra, sucking one nipple into his mouth and then the other. I was wearing a skirt, the soft folds bunched up over my hips, and he slowly ran his hands up my thighs, gripping my flesh.

"You're so soft," he whispered.

"And you're not," I said, my hands moving up and down his chest, learning the hard planes of him.

He grinned and let me pull off his shirt so I could keep touching him. He was all cut edges and hardness. Ink, scars, and man. I kept touching him, wanting more. He was different than Ronin, who was also ink and scars. I loved that I was learning them in different ways, and that this was different than what I had with my husband. This wasn't Ronin, and yet it felt right. This was what Ronin and I had been missing, even if we would have had a perfect future without Kincaid. I knew this only enhanced everything.

Kincaid slowly ran his hands up under my skirt, tugging at my lace panties.

I groaned, rocking myself along his erection.

"Need a condom," he whispered.

I nodded, reaching for my purse. I pulled one out and grinned. "Ronin put this in there a week ago, for just in case. That man is a planner."

Kincaid laughed before he kissed me again, and we kept moving, rocking into one another. I undid his belt, and both of us moved to pull his pants down to his knees. Then he sheathed himself, and I met his gaze, my hand on his shoulder. When he placed himself at my entrance, I slowly, ever so slowly, rotated my hips and lowered myself onto him. He filled me to the point that it was almost too much, and I let out a shuddering breath, needing a moment. He was so deep this way, and it took me a bit to breathe. And then he was kissing me again, his hands on my body as he slowly brought me closer to the edge. When we moved, him thrusting up, me pushing down onto him in the perfect rhythm, I panted, needing more. He played with my breasts before flicking my clit, and then I came, rocking on him, forgetting everything but him and Ronin and what we could be.

Kincaid kept moving, and then he came hard, biting my shoulder as he grunted with his orgasm.

I held onto him, both of us shaking, still partially clothed, and then a pointed cough behind us pulled me out of my thoughts. I looked over my shoulder and grinned.

Ronin leaned against the doorway, shaking his head. "I'm glad I didn't invite Aaron in after he dropped off your car," Ronin said softly.

"Hi, husband," I whispered, not feeling the least bit self-conscious.

Ronin closed the door with a click behind him and strode over to us.

"Do you mind if I join?" my husband asked.

And then Kincaid and I, without saying a word, held up our hands, and the connection snapped into place.

Chapter 8

Ronin

Me: *Are you enjoying your trip?*

Kincaid: *It's a fun project. I should be back in town in the next couple of days. Julia said that you guys were planning on a movie night?*

I smiled as I looked down at my phone. I felt so domestic talking to Kincaid like this. I didn't know where he fit in my relationship with Julia, or in any part of our lives, but we were taking it as slowly as we could, trying to figure out where we were. At least that's what I hoped. In my fears, I imagined Kincaid walking away again, deciding that this was too much for him and that he didn't want to deal with this. Or Julia saying that it was the same for her and she needed space. I wasn't even sure I was allowing myself to think about what I wanted other than acknowledging that I was happy. I was happy with Julia, had always been. She brought out the best in me. But it was as if something had clicked when Kincaid arrived. And not just the anger and betrayal I felt when he first showed up and I thought that he had left because I did something wrong. Alexis had cheated, had left us both long before she'd broken her promises to us. When Kincaid had left without a word soon after, I thought it had been my fault. I hadn't known he'd been pulled away and hurt in the process.

I still wasn't sure what the answers were, or what we would

accomplish, but I hoped that we would find a way to make this work—if that's what the three of us wanted.

Kincaid: *I'm headed out on assignment. In the mood to get this portrait done, and that means we are headed out to the wilderness. I'll have my phone on me, but kiss Julia for me.*

I grinned, shaking my head.

Me: *I can do that. Then you can come and do it yourself.*

Kincaid: *I can do that.*

There were no goodbyes, no professing our feelings. I didn't think we were there yet, and frankly, I didn't know what I felt. I was glad that he didn't say anything.

"You were smiling for a moment, and now you're frowning." I looked up from my chair at Marcus's words, piles of paper all around me, and shook my head.

"Oh, I'm fine. Just thinking."

"Was that Kincaid or Julia?" Marcus asked, a small smile on his face.

I snorted. "You know, I guess I was a little nosy when it came to your relationship with Bristol. I deserve you needling me about my life."

Marcus rolled his eyes. "Yes, because my asking a single question is needling. I've been very restrained when it comes to your love life."

"And I appreciate that," I said honestly. "Mostly because I have no idea what I'm doing, and I'm hoping to hell I don't screw things up."

"If you need to talk, I'm here. Really, any of us are."

"I like how you say 'us' as if you're a Montgomery." I laughed.

"They do just take you in, don't they?" Marcus smiled. "My sisters and their husbands are good for listening, too. If you need advice on anything."

"Julia and I have been married for a while. I think I've got this down."

Marcus threw back his head and laughed, though it wasn't too loud seeing as we were in a library, after all. "Those are famous last words. Nobody ever knows what they're doing when it comes to marriage. We're all figuring it out one day at a time. That's what makes it fun."

"You know, that scares me, but I understand it."

"You're off by the way, it's after five. Go home to your wife. Or Kincaid. Or both. Look at you."

I resisted the urge to flip him off. We might have been in the back of the library, but anyone could walk by at any moment, and that's all we needed, a book club member seeing us flipping each other off and acting like kids rather than librarians with degrees.

"Kincaid's out on a project. I am going home to my wife."

"I will be doing the same in an hour. Have a good night, Ronin. It's good to see you smiling and happy. Just don't let that frown come back."

I shook my head, waved, and headed to my car. I winced as I got in, my leg bothering me. There had been a storm the night before, and I had felt like I was being stabbed with pins and needles until it passed. I hated that I still had pain after all these years. It wasn't as bad as it used to be, but this was a life-altering and never-ending injury. I had constant doctor's visits and fittings to ensure that I was keeping on top of things to avoid any more injuries I could possibly get. And there was no forgetting what had happened to me. No forgetting the pain or the agony or the fire. I wore a symbol of that attack every day.

Same as Kincaid did. I'd felt his scars on his back, had seen them with my own eyes. Julia and I hadn't asked him about them because there was no need. If Kincaid ever wanted to talk about each and every one, we would be there. But we knew what had happened. And that's all we needed to know.

I shifted in my seat and used the controls on my steering wheel to make my way home. When I pulled in, I was tired, a little cranky, and all I wanted to do was lay down on the couch, watch a movie, and rest my eyes.

It had been a long day at the library, the issues with funding and internet outages from the storm piling up. It was only during those last moments when I was texting with Julia and Kincaid that I had felt any real joy for the day.

I loved my job, but it was sometimes exhausting. While it might be something I loved to do, it wasn't what I'd thought to do for my entire life.

I shook myself out of those melancholy thoughts and made my way inside, limping a bit since I had been standing for too long.

Julia was nowhere to be seen, but there was a candle burning, warm and inviting, as well as something in the Crock-Pot. We both worked long hours, and Julia hadn't worked from home today, but I liked that we were figuring out how to feed each other instead of relying on pizza. However, I could have used a pizza tonight.

I got out a beer, popped the top, and took a big gulp, rolling my shoulders back. I should probably sit down, but I wanted to find my wife. I made my way to the back of the house, over the deck that we had built the year Julia moved in. She loved planting, loved gardens, and our backyard was always a work in progress. I knew the gardens reminded her of her parents and her sister, but these were ours, not something they had made together, a thing they had kept her away from.

My hand gripped the beer bottle a little tighter, and I held back a growl. I did not need to think about her parents right now. They weren't worth the energy.

Julia was on her hands and knees, ass in the air as she worked on one of her beds, and my dick twitched, the sight of her luscious curves right in front of me, almost too much to bear.

I held back a groan, or at least I tried. The sound escaped my mouth, and Julia looked over her shoulder, her eyes dancing with laughter.

"I should have known you would walk up as soon as I bent over."

"It's just an invitation for me." I made my way down the deck's ramp, a replacement for the stairs we'd put in a few years ago.

"I'm almost done. I made this random beef burgundy thing that I found on the internet. Hopefully, it doesn't suck."

I couldn't bend down just then, so she stood up, her gaze going to my leg for an instant. She knew I was in pain, and I didn't hide it from her. I didn't hide anything from my wife. She pushed my hair back from my face, kissed me softly, and then took the beer from my hands. She took a long swig and grinned.

"Yummy."

"It is. I needed it after today."

"Bad pain day because of the storms?"

"Pretty much. And I had to be on my feet longer than I planned. I'm fine, just glad we're relaxing tonight."

She ran her hand over the scruff of my beard and kissed me again. "I guess I could always give you a massage."

"With oil?"

"How much porn have you been watching recently?"

"What? I'm just saying, all that oil going everywhere, things get slippery. Hands go places."

She snorted, handed me the beer, and leaned against me. "I need to clean up, but you go take a seat, and then we can work on that massage."

"I don't think I'm getting the oil, am I?"

"As you said, oil gets everywhere. But I promise you might get a happy ending if you play your cards right."

"There she is, the love of my life." I kissed the top of her head and took the bucket of tools from her as she handed them over, her knee pads and other gardening equipment in her hands. "The garden's coming together."

"It is. I have a couple of spots that I need to plant a few things in. But we can head to the nursery together when we hit the season."

"That sounds like a plan. Kincaid was saying that he wanted to get a few stock shots of different foliage. Maybe he should come."

"That would be fun. Very domestic," she said carefully as we put everything away.

I handed her the beer, and she took the final swallow. I shrugged. "Maybe. I think we're figuring this all out."

"I like it, Ronin. I honestly don't know if we would have gone through with our plans to find somebody else for us."

"And then he just showed up." And had nearly flattened me, but we were getting through it. At least, I hoped so.

"He did. And it's scary, and yet not. I don't know why it feels so right, even though it's only been a few weeks."

"We're finding what works for us. Maybe? Because we were who we needed to be all along, but maybe who we need to be, alters as the paths around us change."

"As long as we have each other and don't hurt Kincaid in the process, or ourselves, I think that maybe this could work."

Hope was a beacon in my chest, but I pushed those thoughts away, afraid of hoping too much. "Let's just see what happens. But I like this."

She smiled and kissed me. "Me, too. Now, I need to go get cleaned up. And you need to sit down, mister."

"Whatever you say, ma'am." I reached around and grabbed her butt. "As long as you take care of me later."

"I always take care of you, darling. That's what makes me the best." She left a smacking kiss on my lips before heading into the house. I followed her, shaking my head. I wasn't quite sure how I'd gotten so lucky, but I knew I was beyond fortunate to have her in my life.

I needed to decide what to do about Kincaid. Or perhaps, wait for him to do the decision making.

After Julia's shower, we sat down in the living room, my leg propped up, and we ate dinner, laughed, and just talked about work.

"That business trip's coming up." I went through my mental calendar.

"Yep. Maybe it'll give you and Kincaid some time alone."

I gave her a wry smile. "Maybe."

"Ronin." She paused. "Is it okay that Kincaid and I were together? I mean, you said so, but I don't know. I don't want to mess things up."

I set down my empty plate and gripped her hand. "Everything we're doing is right. We're talking about it, making rational decisions. We're in a relationship—the three of us. That means we pair off. Just because Kincaid and I haven't yet doesn't mean we won't in the future. Things have to be right. Organic."

"And you and Kincaid have enough history that being alone together is something that's going to take time."

A sharp pain slid into me for the barest moment before it faded away. "You're right. But we'll figure it out. No matter what, I'm always yours."

"Same here. But I want to make sure the two of you are happy, as well. And not just surrounding me." I opened my mouth to say something, but she pressed her finger to my lips. "I know you tell me all the time that I am the center, but you're allowed to be in the center, too."

I leaned over and brushed my lips against hers, pulling her hand down between us.

She smiled and kissed me harder.

"How about that massage?" I whispered.

"We can do that." She rubbed her hands down my back and then tugged at my shirt. We were still sitting on the couch, her doing most of the moving because I was settled. And when she deepened the kiss, I groaned, my hands sliding up her shirt. I cupped her breasts, the heavy mounds overfilling my palms.

"I love your tits," I whispered.

"They are pretty fabulous." She laughed before she kissed me again. Hungry, I pushed at her slightly, and then stood up, taking my crutch with me.

"Come on. I want you in the bedroom. All spread out before me so I can feast."

She blushed and led the way, her hips swaying with enough movement that my cock pressed hard against my pants, my mouth watering.

"Damn," I whispered.

She made her way to the bed and crawled away from me, her ass still in the air. And then she sat in the middle, her knees in front of her, and she bit her lip.

"What did you say about feasting?" she asked.

I groaned and moved to the bed, both of us careful not to move too fast. And then I was tugging off her clothes, her doing the same to mine. I glided my body down hers, lapping and licking, nibbling on her skin. And when I was situated between her legs, I spread her so I could see her wetness before I blew cool air over her. She moaned, cupping her breasts, and I lapped at her, sucking and licking. I speared her with two fingers, and she arched, my name on her lips as she came. Just a single touch, and she came.

"Trigger happy," I mumbled against her heat and continued eating my fill.

"Ronin," she whispered.

"That's it, say my name. Keep going."

She came again, a beautiful blush suffusing her skin.

I shifted so I was above her, her legs bracing me for support, and then I met her gaze and slid deep inside. She was warm and tight and gripped me like a glove. I had to hold my breath, trying not to come. Then I leaned over her and began to move. She held me, both of us leisurely moving against each other. This was not routine, but it was known. A new pleasurable sensation wrapped in memory.

This was the woman I loved, the one I had fallen for years ago. We had grown together, finding our peaks and valleys, discovering our hopes and dreams.

When she came again, I couldn't help but follow, my control lost. I pounded into her as I came, my mouth on hers. And then we rolled over, her straddling me so I took the pressure off my good leg.

She continued rocking on me as we both shook with release. I held her close, knowing that this was the woman I loved more than anything.

Our lives might be changing, we may have allowed Kincaid into our circle, and perhaps into our future, but this was still my touchstone. My center.

My Julia.

And I hoped to hell that what we were doing wouldn't force me to lose the one thing in my life I treasured most.

Chapter 9

Kincaid

"I should've worn a tie," I mumbled.

Julia snorted beside me before she ran her hands down my front. I groaned, and she raised a brow.

"You don't need a tie. We're going to Ronin's family's house. They are anything but formal. You know them."

I shook my head, then took her hand in mine before I kissed her palm. Her eyes widened for a second before she gave me a sweet smile.

"I knew them years ago. That doesn't mean I know them now."

"That might be true, but they remember you. Ronin said so."

"Do they remember the fact that I was an asshole?" I grumbled.

"Maybe, but we all have our pasts, and Ronin's family is amazing. They're going to love you."

I shook my head and then moved away from Julia, mostly because if I didn't, I was likely to bend her over the couch and have my way with her. After all, she was wearing a very easy-to-access dress. It practically begged me to ruck up that skirt and slide between those luscious curves.

She raised a brow again, and I had a feeling she knew exactly where my mind had gone.

"Do not think of mussing me up. I cannot go to Ronin's family with sex hair."

"Again," Ronin joked, his hands on his watch as he did the clasp.

"Really?" I asked, intrigued.

"It was one time," Julia said.

"It's been many times, and I'm pretty sure my parents just think you have messy hair."

Julia's face paled, and she shook her head. "No, your mother knows what that hair means. She's had it before."

Ronin froze, and then visibly shuddered. "That's just cruel," Ronin said.

I laughed, loving the interaction.

"Okay, let's go. Time to face the guillotine."

Ronin snorted and then leaned forward, brushing a gentle kiss to my lips. "They aren't that bad. And they know that the three of us are dating. That two of us are married, and you're dating both of us. They know we're a throuple, a triad, whatever label you want to put on it. There's no hiding it."

My shoulders visibly relaxed, even if I was still nervous. "Good. So, I have to ask what they thought about that."

Ronin gave me a look. "They weren't surprised about the idea of me in a relationship with more than one person. They knew I was in one before. Though, they haven't grilled me about it."

"Everything's going to be fine," Julia said, and I had to wonder if she was talking to herself or to me.

We made the quick ride to Ronin's parents' home, with me behind the wheel, and Julia in the back seat. It gave Ronin more room for his leg, and I didn't mind driving. It kept my mind occupied so it didn't go in a thousand different directions about how everything could go wrong and I could fuck this up.

Ronin slid his hand over my knee and squeezed. "Stop stressing. My parents are pretty cool people. They get it."

"How can they get something that I'm just now starting to figure out?" I asked, my voice a whisper.

"How about we say that they understand the fact that we are not in a monogamous heterosexual relationship," Julia said. "They don't need to know every single thing we do, nor every part of our past."

I let out a rough chuckle. "I hope to hell they don't need to know every single thing we do." I raised a brow, and Ronin shook his head, his lip twitching. "What? I'm just saying. Some things people do not need to know. Especially about what I'm going to do to Julia later."

"If it's anything like what my plans are, it should be fine."

I looked over at Ronin and grinned. "We should take notes. Make sure we're on the same page."

"This is not fair," Julia said, squirming in the back seat.

"Life isn't fair, but then you get fucked."

Julia laughed at my horribly crude joke, and I pulled into the driveway.

I had never been to this home, as Ronin's parents had moved in the last decade or so. But it was a nice ranch-style house and a bit unique in the neighborhood since it didn't seem that they had an HOA. Or maybe it was just lax. Everything seemed perfect for the individuals, and their house didn't look like anyone else's. I liked that.

"Okay, let's get in. Everything's going to be fine." Julia leaned forward, kissed my cheek, then Ronin's, and got out of the car.

"She sounds like she's raring to go."

"My parents love her. Considering the pieces of shit her parents are, I'm glad that she has someone."

"She told me some of what happened. I'm surprised that you haven't done anything about it."

Ronin looked out the window to where Julia was waiting and gave me a tight shake of his head. "I don't have time to go into it, but I do what I can. If I could take her away from her parents completely so she never had to deal with them, I would. But that wouldn't help anything. Not when she still loves them."

I understood, far more than I cared to admit. But I pushed those thoughts out of my head, knowing that it wasn't the time to deal with my family drama or Julia's. No, today was the day we dealt with the ones that were okay with this. I didn't want to know what would happen when dealing with the people who *weren't* okay with who we were.

We didn't even have to ring the doorbell. Ronin's mom was suddenly on the front step, her hands in front of her. "You're here. It's been forever."

Ronin rolled his eyes and then made his way over to his mom, hugging her close. "It has been two days since I talked to you on the phone, and we texted all day today while planning this. I saw you what? Three weeks ago?"

"Three terrible weeks. I know you've been busy with work and very new, exciting things in your life, but your mother misses you."

She kissed Ronin's cheek again, then held out her arms for Julia. Julia sank into her hold, and Ronin's mom hugged Julia tightly, kissing her forehead.

"You look amazing. So bright and happy. And this must be the reason behind it."

Ronin's mother looked over and smiled. She appeared slightly older than she had the last time I'd seen her, but she was still stunning. Dark hair, dark eyes, and a wide smile.

"Hello, Kincaid. It's good to see you again." I didn't know what to do with my hands. Should I hold one out for a handshake or hug her? I didn't know. But then she took the choice away from me and pulled me in tight. I awkwardly put my arms around her and patted her back.

"It's good to see you, Mrs. Boston."

"Oh, it's good to see you too, darling. And you know you should call me Rose."

"Rose. I can do that." I paused. "Maybe."

Ronin's mother laughed and took a step back. "Come inside, Gregory is working on the grill in the back." She rolled her eyes just like her son had. "You know men. They need to be all growly and caveman when it comes to the grill. I tried to help, but God forbid I touch fire."

She laughed at Julia, who grinned. "Sometimes, Ronin lets me grill. However, the one time I grilled with the two of them, Kincaid pretty much pushed me out of the way to help out. I've been relegated to the kitchen. Where all women need to be, apparently. Barefoot." She snorted as she said it.

I nearly laughed. "I did not push you."

"No, you didn't push, just put your manly presence in front of the grill and glowered as if it was your territory."

"I like grilling, what can I say?"

"And I'm not that bad," Ronin added. "I let you grill."

"*Let?*" Julia asked. "See? You *let* me grill. As if it isn't our grill, and as if I don't have the option of helping whenever I want."

"I'm never going to win this, am I?" Ronin asked.

"Not even a little," Gregory said as he walked into the house. He looked much like an older version of Ronin, a little wider, gray at the temples.

"I'm glad you're here. Your mother hasn't stopped talking about the fact that she hasn't seen her precious baby boy in far too long."

"It's true," Rose said, putting her clasped hands in front of her. "However, I wasn't nagging."

"Did I say nagging? You inferred nagging. I didn't say that. I've learned."

"So you say," Rose said before she kissed her husband's cheek. Gregory came fully into the living room, hugged Ronin tight, then did the same to Julia, kissing the top of her head. When Gregory took a step towards me, I swallowed hard.

"Sir."

"You can call me Gregory. Just not Greg. You remember how I hate that name."

My lips twitched. "I remember."

I held out my hand, and Gregory shook his head. Disappointment slid through me, but then I was enveloped in the other man's arms, and I took a deep breath before I hugged him back.

"It's good to see you."

"It really is," Rose said as Gregory took a step back. "And we're so sorry about your sister. We met her that once, and she was so sweet. This will be the last time we talk about it if you want, because we're not going to make you talk about anything you don't want to. However, we are glad that you're back."

Ronin's mother said that all in one breath and then leaned into her husband as he tugged her away slightly as if to calm her down.

Julia slid her hand into mine, while Ronin moved to my other side, resting his hand on the small of my back.

It was odd to feel so centered around two people I hadn't expected. But they were there for me, even if I felt like I was freaking out inside.

"Okay, we have a few drinks for you guys, as well as a lovely non-alcoholic concoction that I made up." Rose clapped her hands. "Have whatever you'd like, and if you want water or coffee, you can have that, but know since I haven't been able to be near the grill, I did have fun with the drinks."

Julia laughed, and Ronin and his father gave each other looks. I shook my head and felt oddly at home for the first time in far too long.

We ate ribs and grilled chicken. Baked beans and potato salad, deviled eggs, a green salad, and some type of bacon-wrapped pineapple thing that I knew I would have asked to take home if we hadn't already eaten all of it.

I leaned back in my chair and rubbed my stomach. "I think I'm going to have to work out an extra two hours tomorrow after this dinner."

"Well, isn't that the greatest compliment?" Rose asked, taking a sip of her sparkling cider.

"Seriously, though, I'm so full, I want to curl into a ball and take a nice long nap," Julia said, leaning into Ronin's side. The three of us were on one side of the table, Ronin's parents on the other. I didn't miss the curious look on Gregory's face. I wasn't a hundred percent sure that Gregory was okay with what was going on, but he hadn't said a word about it. Honestly, he outwardly seemed fine with it. It was only every so often that I would catch a glimpse and wonder. I didn't know if it was about the three of us together or if he thought I was breaking up Julia and Ronin's marriage. Or maybe it was because I had left like I had the first time.

Julia reached out and patted my thigh, keeping her hand there after. I put my arm around her chair. It was the three of us, my fingers trailing along Ronin's shoulder as I leaned a little bit closer.

I liked that we felt like a unit, even if I hadn't known exactly how we had gotten here.

This was so different than it was with Alexis.

I hated the idea that her name was even in my head. We had tried being a triad with her, but Ronin and I had seemed more suited, while Alexis hadn't known what she wanted. And when she walked away and hurt us, I figured that my time doing something outside the norm had passed.

And then I fell into myself, into the bottle, and it had taken me far too long to get out again.

Julia squeezed my knee, and I looked over at her and Ronin, who each gave me looks. I shook my head slightly, not wanting them to know what I was thinking about.

The conversation moved to work, art shows, and upcoming weddings and babies of their friends. I didn't know their friends all that well since I had only heard of them in passing, but we had an upcoming dinner with one of Julia's coworkers, a man who was also in a triad. It would be nice to get to know people in a relationship similar to ours, even if no two relationships were exactly the same.

Julia and I helped Rose clean up the table after dinner, all of us in the kitchen laughing while Ronin and his father went to work on the grill.

"Oh, can you get this to Gregory?" Rose said, handing me a glass of ice water. "He always gets headaches at night with the allergies and forgets to stay hydrated."

"Taking care of him still?" I asked, teasing.

"Of course. He's my husband, and he expects me to nag him, even if he's not allowed to say that word anymore."

She winked and went back to washing dishes while Julia dried. Julia smiled at me, and I lifted a little inside, feeling as if this could be something more than just a moment in time.

I moved out to the deck, and because the grill was to the side, Ronin and Gregory didn't see me come up, but I could hear them.

"Are you okay?" Gregory asked.

"Why do you ask?" Ronin's voice was slightly wooden.

I froze, not knowing what to do. I wanted to know what Ronin was going to say, and what Gregory wanted. I might be an asshole for eavesdropping, but I needed to know.

"With whatever's happening with the three of you."

"I don't know, Dad. We're figuring it out."

Gregory let out a breath, and I held mine. "And Julia is okay with this?" Gregory voiced, a bit of a bite to his tone.

Ronin let out an annoyed breath. "Yes. I'd never do anything to hurt my wife. And this was Julia's idea."

I couldn't exactly see them, so I didn't know their body language, but I wanted to walk away, to make things easier. And then Gregory spoke again.

"Okay, that's good. I had to ask because I love you. And I love that little girl in there, too. Just remember there are now three hearts involved. I don't want any of you hurt. Including Kincaid."

I swallowed hard, emotions overwhelming me, and I tried to catch up to my thoughts.

I was deep into this already, and I hadn't meant to be. If I weren't careful, the time to walk away would pass quickly, and we'd all end up hurt. And with Julia and Ronin, I would never forgive myself if I broke them.

I'd never forgive myself if I was selfish and stayed when I wasn't wanted.

Chapter 10

Julia

"How many plants do you need?" Kincaid asked, and I heard the trepidation in his tone. I held back a snort, doing my best not to laugh at him. After all, he was on an afternoon date with Ronin and me, doing something very domestic—plant shopping for my garden.

"I have a setup in mind," I said, pulling out my tablet. "I even drew up my plans, but some areas are filled with what inspires me given what we see. That way, I'm not too disappointed if they don't have the exact blooms I had in mind."

Kincaid gave me a look, and I blushed.

"What?" I asked.

"You amaze me more every day."

My heart flooded with happiness, and I smiled at him. I looked over at Ronin, who had his hands in his pockets. He looked between us, a small smile playing on his face, and, oh, I wished I could read my husband's mind. Kincaid might joke that we could hear each other's thoughts, but not in reality. I wanted to know what my husband was thinking, what he wanted, what he thought of Kincaid every day.

Hopefully, soon, I would figure that out. But for now, we were on a day-date and looking for plants.

"You don't have to pick out anything," I said. "You *do* have to be my heavy labor person, though."

Kincaid groaned. "Great. I'm so excited."

"You don't have to sound too enthusiastic." Ronin shook his head. "This is one of our favorite days, and you're going to get sweaty. *Really* sweaty." Ronin practically groaned when he said it, and I pressed my lips together, holding back a laugh.

"Okay, enough of that. We could play who gets sweatier faster later. For now, we are going to get two of those carts there and start looking for pallets."

"Did she say pallets?" Kincaid asked.

"Oh, she said pallets. Why do you think she and I have been digging out the beds for the past three weeks?"

"I don't know. How full do your gardens get?"

I turned and looked at him, my tablet in my hands. "Pretty full. I love plants. I may be analytical and love science, but I have a green thumb."

"I do not." Kincaid looked down at his hands. "They're pretty black. If I touch anything, it could die. I don't want to be responsible for that."

I snorted. "I don't believe in black thumbs. Just the idea that you need a little more help. And if you do not want to help with digging or planting, you don't have to. You can stand and brood and watch me bend over."

"You know, I don't know about the brooding, but I could definitely watch the bending."

He leaned over and kissed me on the lips, and I was aware that Ronin still had his hand on my hip. Others could see us connected, but I didn't care anymore. We weren't hiding, we hadn't been, but we hadn't been truly open either. Nobody was paying attention to us, and I was grateful for that. *One small step at a time*, I told myself.

Kincaid seemed to realize what he was doing and pulled away, blushing. "I'm sorry."

"Don't be." I gave him my free hand, squeezed his, then leaned over and kissed Ronin on the lips. "We're doing this, right?" I asked, far more scared than my tone let on.

But Ronin seemed to read my mind, even though I had told myself he couldn't. "We are. Now, come and tell us where you want us."

"Oh, so many wicked ways. I could have fun with that." We laughed, and the three of us moved our way through the nursery, our carts filling up quickly.

"These are beautiful," I said, leaning over a small garlic bush. "They get little purple blooms."

"It's garlic?" Kincaid asked.

"Yes, come and smell."

He did and wrinkled his nose. "That's not too floral."

"No, it's garlic, but they're pretty, and my bees will like them. And there's this bottle brush over here that I want for that back corner. We lost a couple of trees in the blizzard that hit us hard over the winter, and this one should be hardy enough."

We went through my list, both of my men straining their muscles as they moved everything for me. I tried to lift flowers and other things, but they kept nudging me gently out of the way, saying they could handle it. And if I got to watch my men in tight T-shirts lifting heavy things and looking sexy as hell? I was a very happy girl.

"Are we going to have enough room in your truck?" Kincaid asked, and I grinned.

"Yes, we'll make it work. And if not, we'll call one of our friends, and they can bring one of their cars, too. But we've done this before."

"Okay, if you say so."

We turned the corner to get our last set of blooms, and I froze, Kincaid nearly running into me as I looked at the people in front of us. Ronin quickly put his hand in mine in a reassuring way, and I knew I should run. I should walk away before the couple in front of me turned and saw us.

I couldn't. This was happiness. I was finally breathing and no longer thinking and wondering about the what-ifs. I was finally letting myself be because while I had been happy with Ronin before, so happy that I could burst, and knew that he was my future and everything would be fine, it wasn't complete. And then Kincaid showed up, and something clicked. It felt like this was the path we were supposed to be on.

With one turn of the corner, all of that fell away, and all I could do was look at the couple in front of me. I couldn't walk away. Couldn't hide from this.

I should have known they would be here. It was the nursery's first day, and the place was packed—people laughing and busy, their pallets full.

Of course, my mother and father would be here to get stuff to work on Taylor's garden.

Taylor's. Never truly my mother's. Nor my father's or mine.

I missed my sister so damn much, and I hated that whatever garden they built wouldn't bring her back. And neither would anything my mother did.

They finally turned, my father going sheet-white as my mother's lips pursed.

"Hello, Mom. Dad."

Kincaid froze at my side, finally realizing why I was acting so weirdly. Ronin stood on my other side, keeping me steady.

He was always that way—my rock. I had been afraid that by doing what we were with Kincaid, I might lose him. But in this moment, I knew I wouldn't. We would stand even stronger together. I just needed to get through this. Whatever *this* was.

"Mom, you remember Ronin." It was weird introducing my husband to them as if they hadn't met him a dozen times or more before. They looked at me, possibly wondering why I was here. I didn't know *what* they were thinking. I'd never been able to read them.

"And this is Kincaid."

My mother looked at how Kincaid hovered near me, his stance protective, and then her gaze darted between Ronin and Kincaid, her eyes narrowing.

She knew. At least, she had some semblance of knowing. She would never truly understand what we felt because we were still figuring that out ourselves. But she would put a spin on it, a taint, assume that I wasn't good enough.

Because I wasn't Taylor. I wasn't the girl she had chosen.

I hated that she was ruining this day. That she ruined so many memories for me.

And she hadn't even spoken yet.

"You're parading it then, are you?" my mother whispered, looking over her shoulder as if someone could see us or hear her.

We were in public, of course, people *could* see, but nobody was paying attention. It was the opening day of the season. Everybody had their own lives and landscaping to worry about. But my mother never understood.

"You mean that I'm planting my garden? Yes, Kincaid's here to help Ronin and me. You're welcome to look at what I plant."

My mother stared at me. "Mrs. Smith told me that she saw you and these two at the grocery store, and that you were acting in your ways. Yet I didn't believe it. I knew you always had your tastes, your proclivities, but with two? No, I don't want this. Don't come to see us, don't talk to us. I'm done. I'm done pretending."

I took a step back, but Kincaid and Ronin were there to steady me.

"Excuse me, you don't know me, but you're going to want to stop talking to her like that."

I briefly closed my eyes at Kincaid's words, then muttered under my breath, "Don't."

"No, he should. I'm kind of tired," Ronin said. "We're trying to go about our day. If you could move out of the way so we can move on, that'd be great. We're working on our garden. The one for our family."

"You always were a whore," my mother spat. "You were off with your girlfriend instead of at home where you should have been when we lost Taylor. You weren't even there to say goodbye."

And there it was, the real reason my mother hated me. She didn't truly hate my choices because she didn't actually care about me.

I had finally taken a moment for myself to go out with Angela, a girl I hadn't seen again after that night. My mother had been the one to tell me to leave the house, that I needed to breathe. Though maybe that's what *she* had needed.

I hadn't been there when Taylor took her last breath. We hadn't even made it to hospice.

I would never forgive myself for not being there, and it had taken me a long time to figure out who I was and what I wanted because of that.

"No." I held out my hands, my tablet in one, and blocked the men from moving forward. "We're not going to do this. You can think whatever you want, but I'm done. I think I tried a little too hard for too long. I don't need to anymore. Good luck with the gardens that I will never be a part of or see. I'm glad that you have something of Taylor there, but I know when and where I'm not wanted. And you will stay away, too. You'll respect my choices, even though you never have before."

People *were* looking now, but I couldn't care anymore. I was so tired.

"Julia, let's not do this here," my father said. He surprised me. He never spoke directly to me. Why would he bother? He was dead inside for more reasons than just the loss of my sister.

"I'm done now. You are not going to ruin this garden like you ruined what I felt for the one at your home. You're not going to ruin anything anymore. I loved you once, Mom. And I might still. But you can't take back what you've done. You can't. I won't allow you to tarnish the memories of my sister anymore. Think what you will of me, but I'm done."

And then I raised my chin and moved past her. My mother didn't even bother to move out of the middle of the walkway. Somehow, Kincaid and Ronin followed me, the carts still full of what our future could be.

"Do you need me to go get the truck?" Kincaid asked, and I shook my head before Ronin could answer.

"Thank you both for standing up for me, but I'm going to get these flowers, and then we are going to go plant what we can today. I will have an amazing garden because I refuse to let her ruin this, too."

I looked up at Ronin, who leaned down and kissed me hard on the mouth. "I love you, wife of mine."

We were off in the corner, no one paying attention to us anymore, and I was grateful. I might've pretended that I could handle being the center of attention, but I really didn't want to be.

And then Kincaid kissed me hard on the mouth just like Ronin had, and I leaned into him, wanting to cry.

But I was done doing that.

No amount of prostrating or pretending could bring Taylor back. All I could do was live in her memory and try to be the best person I could. And perhaps fall in love more than once with a man who made me feel like I could have a future.

"Let's go home," I whispered.

"Yes, let's go home. However, that's the last time she gets to speak to you that way. I held back for long enough," Ronin growled.

"I know you did. And I'm grateful."

"She's very lucky I do not hit women."

I smiled at my husband, shaking my head. "I wanted to hurt her, too, but then she'd probably sue, and we'd have to deal with the legalities."

"I know people. I could probably get us out of that," Kincaid said dryly.

"Thank you both, but we are not ruining this day. It's all about flowers and me seeing you sweaty. Not about my weird family and broken promises." My voice cracked a bit, and I held up my hands again, not letting Kincaid come near me. "I can cry later. First, we pay for these, I watch you load them into the truck, and then we plant. I'll have a very good cry later."

"I'm sure we can find ways to get your mind off crying," Kincaid said, giving Ronin a wicked look.

I pressed my lips together, holding back a laugh. I'd just broken something important, but perhaps it had been shattered long ago. Now, I was finally living up to who I needed to be.

And that was with Ronin, the man I loved more than anything. And perhaps also with the man we hadn't realized we'd been missing in our marriage.

Chapter 11

Ronin

"You ready?" I asked, pushing my hand through my hair as I looked at my reflection in the mirror. I hardly recognized myself, a new, odd glint to my eyes that meant something had changed. I hadn't been unhappy before. I hadn't been sad or missing anything. But now that Kincaid was back? And the idea of what I thought I'd lost had been proven untrue, things felt newer. More cemented.

I knew Julia felt the same because we often talked about it, but I didn't know how Kincaid felt. And tonight was not the night to get into that conversation.

Kincaid looked at me, his face serious in his reflection. "I think so. But are you sure that it's okay I'm going?" he asked, his voice gentle.

"Yes. It's guys' night. The Montgomery men, or at least those connected to the Montgomerys, are going out. And they invited me. And because you're with me, you're invited, too." I paused. "And once they get to know you, you'll be invited even without me."

That made Kincaid snort. "Since I work from home usually, or at least on my own, I don't have any friends here other than you and Julia." He frowned. "I don't know what that says about me."

"It says we're living in an age where it's harder to make friends as adults. But don't worry, you'll like these guys."

"I've met Ethan before," Kincaid added.

"And you'll like his brothers, Ethan's husband Lincoln, and Bristol's husband, Marcus. I work with him."

Kincaid rolled his eyes. "I know. You've already given me the complete breakdown of the family tree. At least the ones that live in this city."

"I wanted to make sure you knew what was going on," I said, shrugging. "There are a lot of them, and they can be intimidating. I didn't want you to be intimidated."

"With all the crap that you and I have been through, Ronin, I don't think a single family will intimidate me."

That made me snort. "Apparently, you haven't met the rest of the Montgomerys. Your tune will change."

"I don't know if you're trying to make me feel better about meeting them or trying to scare me. You're sending conflicting messages."

I shrugged. "Possibly. That's my prerogative."

"I'm going to be singing that song for a while."

That made me laugh. "I haven't heard it in ages." I leaned forward, kissed Kincaid on the lips like we had been doing it for years rather than only recently again, and knew that soon this honeymoon bliss of when we didn't talk about anything serious would have to come to an end. We'd soon have to make decisions and talk because things were getting serious without us even thinking about it. I didn't want Julia to get hurt because we weren't talking. I didn't want to get hurt either, but it was easier to worry about the love of my life than myself. That way, I didn't have to think too deeply.

"Where are we meeting?" he asked.

"A local sports bar. It's kind of nice, all-leather interior, and doesn't smell like ass."

That made Kincaid laugh. "That's always good. We aren't young anymore. I don't need to hang out with a bunch of dude-bros and scream at the television over a sports program I actually don't care about."

"I bet if it were hockey, you would care."

"Of course, I would care. But we're not watching hockey, are we?" he asked.

"No, but I bet we can get down to an Avalanche game if you want."

"That'd be fun. But I know between Julia being out of town for this project and her upcoming big one, and my next out-of-town thing, we're going to be a little busy."

I shrugged. "We've got time. We'll pin it in the map for the future."

Kincaid didn't say anything about that, and I ignored the hurt I felt. Maybe he was just thinking and wasn't worried about the fact that he wasn't making promises beyond tomorrow.

I needed to stop overthinking things, but that's what I did. I overthought, and I got myself into shitty situations. I hated the idea that I didn't know what was happening with Kincaid and my relationship with Julia. Let alone what was happening in the offshoots of that relationship.

We got in the car, and Kincaid turned on *My Prerogative*. I closed my eyes, holding back laughter as Kincaid sang off-key, and we made our way to the bar.

"You're welcome to have a drink tonight," Kincaid said, and I frowned.

"Shit. I didn't even think."

Kincaid just laughed. "I'm fine going into a bar. I've done it before."

"I didn't tell the others anything about your past. It wasn't my right."

"And I'm grateful for that. No one needs to know what I've done. They just need to know *the me* now. You can know," he added. "You and Julia. But the others? No, I don't know them well enough or at all for that matter to dive into my deepest, darkest secrets."

"We can go somewhere else. I'll tell them I'm not in the mood."

"No, I'm fine. I'll be the designated driver. It's what I'm good at."

"If things get hard, we'll leave. I promise."

Kincaid's eyes went dark, and he looked down at my crotch. "If things get hard for you, just let me know."

That made me laugh outright.

"That's one way to put it."

"I'm just saying, I'm right here when you need me."

"We'll have to see what comes up later."

Kincaid snorted at my horrible joke, and we made our way in.

The place was a bar, but it was more of a lounge that happened to have a bar. The Montgomerys were at the other end, most of them drinking soda with a couple of beers on the table. I knew they didn't know that Kincaid was an alcoholic, but none of the Montgomerys went full tilt when it came to drinking anyway. Still, I should have thought about the whole bar scene. I had just been so worried about Kincaid and our future and him meeting my friends that I hadn't thought about the important shit.

I needed to get my head out of my ass and worry about what was in front of me rather than what I couldn't fix.

Kincaid stopped me before we made our way to the corner and put his hand on the back of my neck. "Stop it. I'm fine. I'm glad that you didn't think of it right away. It means it's not the first thing you think about when you look at me."

"I think about a lot of things when I look at you," I whispered, baring myself more than I wanted.

Kincaid gave me a dark look before he shook his head, and we made our way to where the others were.

Ethan saw us first and grinned. "Hey there. You're here. We thought you got lost. Or, you know *busy...*" He winked, and his husband rolled his eyes.

"Very subtle, Ethan."

"What? I'm just saying." Ethan grinned.

"What he isn't adding is the fact that they just arrived before you because they were *busy,*" Liam said dryly, and I laughed.

"Everyone, this is Kincaid. Kincaid, this big, strapping inked man in the corner is Liam. You know Ethan, that's his husband Lincoln, and Marcus is in the corner over there. And, sitting in front of you is Aaron, the baby of the family."

Aaron flipped us off. "Excuse me, not the baby."

"Whatever you say," the brothers said at the same time, and I laughed, Kincaid joining me.

Aaron continued. "We got a big booth since the bigger table is already taken with a bachelor party."

"Bachelor party?" I asked, frowning. "Most people don't come here for bachelor parties."

"No, I think they just wanted something casual," Liam added.

"Yeah, not everybody needs strippers and blow for their send off," Aaron said.

Kincaid just shook his head. "I'm glad to know we're not getting that here. Julia would probably kick our asses."

"Dude, *I* would kick your ass," I said, and Kincaid just grinned.

"What can I get you guys to drink?" a waiter said as he walked toward us. He was a slender guy, probably in his early twenties, and hot. I noticed that half the men at the table checked the guy out, and he did the same. Liam just met Marcus's gaze, and they shook their heads, grinning.

We were all taken, but we weren't dead.

"I'll just take a Coke." Kincaid smiled.

"Is Pepsi okay?" the man asked.

Liam shook his head while Kincaid laughed. "No, how about a club soda with lime then."

"I had a feeling you were going to say that." The waiter winked at my man. "I think we're switching to a Coke distributor soon. Nobody ever likes Pepsi here."

"Because it's sacrilege," Kincaid said, and the waiter kept looking at him.

I cleared my throat pointedly, and the waiter blushed, saw the way that Kincaid's hand was on my thigh, and had the grace to look a little ashamed of his overt flirting.

"Anyway, what can I get for you?"

I held back a smile. "I'll take the same as him."

"You can get anything you want," Kincaid whispered. "Remember, I'm the DD."

"I'm fine. I want a clear head."

Our waiter nodded. "Two club sodas with limes. Any refills?"

"We're all good on beer, but if you could bring a round of waters? That'd be good." Marcus looked at everybody as we nodded.

"Sounds great."

"We're going to order appetizers and meals soon," Aaron added at the crestfallen look on the guy's face that he'd almost hidden. "I promise we won't take up your table for club soda and water."

The young twenty-something blushed again. "Sorry, didn't mean to show the inner workings of my mind."

"Hey, we've all been in customer service before. At least most of us," Aaron said dryly as he looked over at Liam. That's when I remembered that Liam had been a model when he was a teenager, so there had been no waiting tables for him.

"We're not going to screw you over," Kincaid added.

"That's good," the kid said, his voice cracking likely because Kincaid said, "screw."

The guy left, and we all looked at each other and laughed.

"You know, I am used to being the man that any waiter and waitress fawns over," Liam said dryly, "but you bring ginger here, and I'm chopped liver."

I looked over at my redheaded man and snorted. "He does have that effect on people."

"And you're too pretty for your own good," Ethan said to his brother, his eyes twinkling. "It's good that you're learning a little humility, Liam."

"You guys are ridiculous," I said on a laugh, and we all sank into a comfortable conversation about work, kids, and life. Kincaid fit in easily, and it was like he had been with the group for years. Hell, I was still new to this group through Marcus, and yet they made me feel like family. We ate wings and a bunch of goodness that was probably horrible for us, but it didn't matter. We just had a good time. And when the evening naturally came to an end, everybody heading home to their significant others, Kincaid drove me back, and I tangled my fingers with his on the way, feeling like a million bucks.

"Julia should be calling in a bit," I said absentmindedly, looking down at the time.

"Good. I haven't heard her voice in over a day now."

I smiled. "It's going to be weird not having her in my bed tonight."

Kincaid gave me a look, his mouth twitching. "If you need me to warm your bed, darling, I can do that for you."

I laughed. "I wasn't very subtle, was I?" I asked.

"No, but that's why I like you."

We made our way into the house right as Julia called. I tapped the cell, and her face popped up onto the screen. I smiled, relief filling me.

"Hey there," I whispered, my voice a purr.

She just grinned. "Hi there, boys. Did you guys have fun tonight?" she asked. "Honestly, I'm surprised you aren't still out with the Montgomerys."

"We all called it an early night. We have people to be with."

"Good," she whispered, and then she looked over my shoulder. "Did you have fun tonight, Kincaid?"

"The Montgomerys are a hoot. I can see why you guys are friends with them."

"Just wait till you hang out with the women."

"That may scare me."

"What's on the agenda tonight?" she asked, and I looked over at Kincaid, swallowing hard. "Uh-huh. On that note, you guys have fun," she said on a laugh. "Kiss each other for me. Have a blast, and don't think too hard."

"Stay safe," Kincaid whispered.

"I love you, babe."

"I love you, too." She was looking at me, but I had a feeling she wasn't speaking only to me. However, since we didn't know exactly where Kincaid stood, Julia and I were very careful about what we said.

"I'll see you in two days," I whispered.

"Two very long days. Have fun tonight. We'll talk tomorrow about the trip. But I'm tired, and you guys need this time."

She hung up before I could say anything, and I just shook my head.

"That woman is far too observant for her own good."

"True, but it's why I love her."

One of the many reasons I loved her.

"You're lucky, Ronin."

"I'm the luckiest damn man in the universe, and I know it."

I smiled softly. "Anyway, I want to take a shower. It's been a long day, and I feel gross. Do you want to join me?"

"I think I can help you wash your back," Kincaid whispered, and I swallowed hard, my cock filling.

We made our way to the bathroom, and I did my best to act as if I weren't freaking the fuck out. But I was. This was my first time alone with Kincaid. Oh, we'd been together numerous times, each of us taking different positions and different ways to love one another. But this was the first time Julia wasn't between us, or near us.

It was a moment.

And I knew that it would mean something. I just hoped to hell we didn't fuck it up.

We didn't need to say much else, both of our breaths coming faster, heavier as we stood in the large bathroom area. There was a tub off to the side where I would sit with Julia to play, or where she could soak. But the shower was wide enough and ADA compliant, with a large bench where I could sit down and not have to worry about falling.

Kincaid lowered his head and kissed me softly before pulling away, leaving me wanting. He turned on the hot water, and then we slowly stripped each other, careful with one another. He helped me into the shower, the showerhead angled away from the seat so he could help me with my prosthesis. I gently pulled it off, and he put it out of the spray, my trust in him great.

He looked at me, storm clouds crossing his gaze and shook his head.

"What?" I asked, not feeling self-conscious in the least.

"I hate that you were hurt. I'm always going to hate that."

I nodded. "You have just as many scars as I do," I whispered. "I get to be just as angry."

"Then let's make sure we don't focus on it tonight."

"That, I can do," I whispered, and then he leaned down and kissed me again. I moaned, the water now moving over us as he adjusted the head before he came back to me. Water sluiced over us, and I moaned again, needing more.

He simply kissed me before going down to his knees and kissing my chest, my stomach before gripping me.

His palms were callused, his fingers firm as he encircled me, pumping. He met my gaze, and then he lowered his mouth to me. I groaned, the heat of him enveloping my dick.

He swallowed me, humming along the length of my cock as he licked and pleasured me. He cupped my balls, rolling them in his palm before he hollowed his cheeks, doing something with his tongue that made me lose focus. And then I was coming, my hand tugging on his hair as I tried to pull him away, but he didn't seem to care. Instead, he hummed against the tip of my dick as he swallowed every last drop. And then he stood up, wiped his mouth, and went for a loofah. He added soap and slowly washed me, not saying a word. But his gaze never left mine as he gently took care of me. And then he handed me the loofah and more soap, and I did the same to him, paying extra special attention to his cock. I tugged, squeezed, worked him to near completion before he pulled away to remove the shower head attachment, rinsing us both off. He turned off the water, got a fluffy towel, and dried us both.

Before I could reach for my crutch or anything I needed, he somehow picked me up, and I wrapped my leg around him, holding him tight.

"You're going to fucking drop me," I whispered. My dick was already hard again, pressed against his stomach, his cock pulsing against mine.

"I've got you, Ronin. I promise."

I kissed him again, and he slowly made his way to the bedroom. He positioned me on the bed before he knelt before me, focused on my cock again. I reached for him, needing him, but he shook his head before he reached into the dresser drawer for some lube and a condom. He sheathed himself and then went to work on me, his fingers probing then stretching me in the best way possible. I moaned, running my hands up and down his body as he worked me, preparing me for him. And when he entered me, my leg up near my shoulder, him slowly working his way in and out of me, I groaned.

"Hold yourself, squeeze yourself, make yourself come."

I did as he instructed, squeezing hard, moving fast as he fucked me, both of us panting and needing. He moved hard, no care, far rougher than he ever was with Julia, and I couldn't help but moan, needing this man in front of me.

And when he pumped hard, slamming into me one last time until he groaned, coming, I spurted all over my chest, coming in pants right along with him.

I looked up at him, swallowed hard, and licked my lips.

"Jesus Christ," I whispered.

"I'm not done with you yet," Ronin replied and kept moving before he leaned down and kissed me, playing with me.

Later, we held each other, both cleaned up once more, and I just leaned into the man I had once loved, the man I was pretty sure I loved again.

I didn't say anything. I wasn't sure I could. But as Kincaid's breaths evened out and he fell into slumber, I wondered what would happen if I told him I loved him. If Julia and I said we wanted more.

I was afraid that, somehow, I wasn't going to be enough. Somehow, we wouldn't be enough. That Kincaid would walk away again just like he had before. I didn't want to think about that, but I couldn't help it.

And so, I didn't sleep. I held him close, wishing this could last forever, and knowing it might not ever happen.

Chapter 12

Kincaid

"I'm way too full," Julia said, leaning back in her seat. I grinned, shaking my head. We were at a nice restaurant, one that served various Mediterranean dishes, and I had eaten probably twice as much as Julia, and I was just as stuffed. But Julia pressing out her little belly, acting as if she could roll away just made me laugh. Ronin snorted and took a sip of his club soda before reaching out with his fork to take the last piece of beef off her plate.

"Yummy," he mumbled.

"I was saving that." Julia groaned and closed her eyes. "Okay, I lied. I can't eat any more."

I laughed, pushing my plate away. "I'm full, too. I was going to get dessert, but I think that's better left for home."

Ronin met my gaze, his eyes going dark. I laughed.

"I meant actual dessert. But that, too."

Julia laughed, rubbed her stomach, and then leaned forward, elbows on the table. "This is nice. I'm glad the three of us are out on a date that has nothing to do with me cooking."

"You know I can always do the cooking," I said.

"Yes, if I want grilled cheese, then I will totally come to you," Julia said dryly.

"Ouch," I said with a laugh. "Just hit me, why don't you."

"I would, but I'm too full to move."

"And we all know that I'm only good on the grill." Ronin shook his head. "But Julia's right. I'm glad the three of us are out. It's a good date," he added. "Come on, let's head home." Ronin met both Julia's gaze and mine.

It wasn't lost on me that he'd said "home," a house I didn't live in.

I just smiled and tried not to let my thoughts show. Because I didn't know what I was thinking to begin with. This wasn't what I had come for. I had wanted to see Ronin, to apologize. And, honestly, just to see him. Never in my wildest dreams had I thought he'd take me back. Let alone with his wife.

And if I let myself truly believe in anything, I knew I felt something more than just attraction for Ronin and the woman he loved.

The woman that I could love.

I wouldn't let myself think too hard on that, though. Because if I did, I'd make a mistake.

I'd made too many mistakes already, and I refused to make more. I did not want to hurt Ronin again, and I wouldn't hurt Julia.

She was a bright light, Ronin's center, and was quickly becoming mine.

It was hard to think about a future when I had spent so many years wallowing in the past. I was better, at least I told myself that I was. But it wasn't easy to remember who I needed to be. And most of the time, I didn't feel like I was that man at all.

We made our way out of the restaurant, and I got into the driver's seat, Ronin helping Julia into the back seat. They kissed softly before she slid in and put her hands on my shoulders as I started the car.

"You know I'm always happy to drive," she whispered, kissing my cheek.

I looked over at her and raised a brow that I wasn't sure she could see. "My car, I drive."

She let out a puff of air. "Men."

"Sorry, you've got two of us now. You're going to have to deal with it."

Julia grinned behind me, at least from what I could see in the rearview mirror, and I let the comment slide over me. Did she have two men? We had slipped into these roles as they were meant for us, and yet I wasn't sure how I'd gotten here. I needed to roll with the punches and not overthink things, but that wasn't who I was. And from the way Ronin was staring at me, I knew that wasn't who he was either.

I drove us back to their place—*not home*, I reminded myself—and pulled into the driveway as we talked about going over to Ethan, Holland, and Lincoln's house for dinner the next week.

"Do you think you can make it?" Julia asked.

"I don't know. What's the date again?"

She rattled off the date as we began the walk inside, and I froze, nearly tripping over my feet.

"Fuck," I mumbled.

They looked at me.

"What?" Ronin asked, his voice careful.

"What time is it?" I asked, looking down at the clock. "Okay, it's still early enough on the West Coast." I looked up at them and shook my head. "Today's my mom's birthday. I completely forgot." I had been so far in my own head, I had forgotten my own mother's birthday. I wasn't sure she wanted to hear from me, she never really did, but I had to try.

Julia frowned. "Oh, no. Okay, I'm going to add it to my calendar so we know for the future."

I ignored the little pang I felt, wondering where that had come from, and shook my head. "I'm going to call her. You mind if I stand out here on the porch?"

"No, you should come in. We'll give you privacy. Come on in," Julia repeated, tugging me inside.

I let her move me, aware that Ronin was studying my face, worry etched there. But I had to ignore it.

I pulled up my mother's contact information and hit call, hoping to hell she answered. It was actually my dad who answered, my mom not bothering to pick up. Not that I knew that for sure, but she'd done it in the past, and I wouldn't blame her for keeping to type.

"You didn't need to call," my dad said, his voice gruff.

I swallowed hard, aware that Ronin and Julia were leaving me alone so I could do this in private. They knew I had problems with my family, that my parents blamed me for my sister's death. But hell, I blamed myself just as much as they did. Still, my parents were venomous about it.

And there was nothing I could do, except keep trying. And yet, hadn't I been the one to help Julia stop trying with her parents? I didn't like those parallels, so I pushed them from my mind. They weren't exactly the same. And not enough time had passed.

"I just wanted to wish Mom a happy birthday."

"You almost missed it, so it's clearly not a big deal."

"Either I missed it, and you care. Or I missed it, and you were glad that I didn't call," I blurted out, and then could've rightly kicked myself.

"Don't take that tone with me. Your mother doesn't want to talk to you. And you know why. She should be here," my father said, and I knew he wasn't talking about my mom.

"I know," I whispered, my voice low.

"Stop calling. She doesn't want to talk to you. And frankly, neither do I." He hung up then, leaving me staring at the phone, wondering why I even tried.

My throat burned, and I knew I didn't want a drink, but I needed to talk to somebody. I looked up at Ronin and clenched my teeth. "I thought you were going to give me space."

"I tried, but your voice carries."

"I'm sorry," Julia whispered from behind him.

I let out a snort. "It's not important. But I've got to go."

"Kincaid, we can talk about this."

I shook my head. "No, I made a mistake. I'm not ready for this."

Julia looked as if I had slapped her, but Ronin just raised his chin. "You mean this conversation? Or this relationship?"

I let out a laugh that held no humor. "*Everything.* I wasn't ready. And if I stay, I'll just hurt you guys. I'll ruin you like I ruin everything else. I need to go to a meeting. Do you understand that? I'm an alcoholic. And I don't need a drink, but I do need to talk to someone."

"Okay," Julia put in, raising her hand and extending it as if to touch me. "You can do that. We'll drive you."

"No, I'm fine."

"You're not fine," Ronin bit out. "You can talk to us, too, you know?"

"I can't. Just let me go."

Julia moved forward. "Call us when you get out of your meeting."

I looked at her and shook my head. "I shouldn't. I can't. This was nice, but if I stay, I'll only break things more. And I don't want you two to end up getting hurt because I can't handle shit. Thank you for everything, but I need to go."

"Kincaid," she whispered.

"No," Ronin put in, his voice brittle. "Let him go. He needs to go to a meeting. And he can."

"But, Ronin…" she began.

"No, just let him go. I get that he needs to get some help and I'd never, *ever* keep him from that, but he's running, too. Holding Kincaid back is futile. Isn't it?" Ronin asked, that same pain I had seen years ago etched onto his features now.

I only nodded before I turned and walked away, knowing I was probably making the worst mistake of my life, but doing the only thing I could—saving the people I knew I loved, and facing the mortality I tried not to look directly in the face.

Chapter 13

Julia

"Did you sleep?" I asked, my voice hollow.

"No. I don't think either of us did."

I looked over at my husband, my heart breaking. "He left," I whispered. Everything felt so empty and covered in shades of gray. "I didn't think he'd actually leave."

"He didn't want to lean on us, didn't want to show that. While I get it, he still left."

"Ronin, we need to go to him. He needs us."

Ronin scoffed. "No, he doesn't. He never needed anyone."

"You're lying to yourself because it hurts," I snapped. "You don't believe that any more than I do. You're trying to protect yourself, and me. But all you're doing is hurting inside. Kincaid needs us." I knew I was about to say something that could change everything. Could break everything. "I love him, Ronin. I love him so much. Just like I love you. And I can't watch him walk away."

Ronin's face shuttered, and I felt like I was falling. As if I'd said too much and made another mistake.

"Julia…" he began, and I moved away, not letting him touch me.

"I shouldn't have told you that. Not when you weren't ready. I'm sorry. I didn't mean to fall in love with someone else, but it happened.

Though it doesn't negate what I feel for you. I thought the three of us were working, that we were finding a way to make a family. And yet, that wasn't the case. He left, and you're just letting him walk away forever."

"Julia, he left once before."

"But he came back," I corrected, swallowing hard.

"He still left. Again."

"Because he needed to go to a meeting, something he had to do on his own. And we needed to let him. But now, we need to go to him and tell him and show him how we feel. Before we do that, though, you need to tell *me* how you feel. Because if we're not on the same page in this, then we're not doing it right. And we are always on the same page, Ronin."

"I..." He trailed off.

"Ronin."

"What if we're not enough?" he asked, and my heart broke for him. I went to him then, cupped his face, and kissed him softly, needing him, loving my husband more than anything.

"Stop it. This isn't what we do. He's hurting, we all are. But together? We're going to make this work. How do you feel about Kincaid?"

"You know how I feel," my husband whispered.

"Tell me. I need to hear the words."

"I love him. And I love you. I think I've always loved him."

"And I knew that." My eyes filled with tears. "We need to get him back. He's hurting, but we were both hurting before, and he held onto us. Now, it's our turn to do that for him. Relationships are hard, and they suck sometimes, and it feels like there's never going to be a way to happiness. But then you get there, and everything is bliss. You and I are proof of that. And I have enough love inside me for both of you. And I know you do, too. Let's make sure he understands that."

"I think I love you more now than I did when I first met you."

"Love is allowed to grow, hearts to beat harder with each passing breath. You have to go get our man. And show him that he's not allowed to leave when things get tough." I slapped Ronin hard on the arm, and he winced playfully.

"What was that for?"

"Because you're not allowed to brood and push me away when you get angry."

"Then you're not allowed to tell me to shut up so you can wallow."

I narrowed my eyes. "I don't do that all the time."

"We each have our own issues," Ronin said with a soft laugh. "But you're right, let's go get our man."

And then he kissed me hard, and I sank into him, wrapping my arms around his shoulders.

"I love you, Ronin."

"I love you with every inch of my soul. And I know it's wrapped around Kincaid, as well, and life isn't going to be easy. But I feel like I can do anything with you at my side."

"That was a part of your vows to me," I whispered, blinking away tears.

"It was. One day, I think we should make sure we have vows for Kincaid, too."

My heart skipped a beat, and I grinned. "We just need to make sure that we're so irresistible that he can't walk away."

Ronin cupped my face and kissed me again. "I think you could do that all on your own."

"The two of us together? Irresistible."

* * * *

I sucked in a breath as we pulled into Kincaid's driveway. We weren't there often, as it always just made more sense for all of us to gather at our house, but I felt like this could be another part of our home if we kept it.

I hated the idea that Kincaid was here all alone, brooding, not letting us hold him. But that was about to change. He would have to deal with us.

I was a little out of breath as I moved to the front door, Ronin at my side. I rang the doorbell even as Ronin knocked, and I grinned.

"He's not going to be able to say no to us."

Kincaid opened the door, dark circles under his eyes, gray sweatpants riding low on his hips. He wore nothing else, his scars bright in the sunlight. "I knew you two would be here eventually," Kincaid said and moved back to let us in. I looked into his eyes, and he shook his head. "I'm fine. I went to a meeting. Talked it out. I'm not drinking."

"I didn't think you would," I said honestly.

"Although I am a little miffed that you didn't talk to us," Ronin grumbled. And then he held up a hand before either Kincaid or I could say anything. "But I understand why you didn't. However, I want you to know that you walking away from us like that? It can't happen all the time. We each have our issues, and we're going to have to figure out how to work through them. Together."

"You guys keep talking like there's a big future coming," Kincaid said, looking between the two of us. "But do you think this can work with the three of us? A future where we don't fuck up, and we live in bliss and all of that shit?"

I shook my head at the vulgarity, knowing Kincaid needed it to put up barriers. "You deserve happiness. Maybe we can be the ones to find it with you. But you deserve forgiveness and hope, too. And I want to be part of that."

Ronin nodded. "So do I."

"How do you see this working?" Kincaid asked softly.

"However we want it to," I said. "Ronin is my husband, but you're mine, too. We don't need titles or legally binding papers to make us who we are. But there can be promises, and a future mapped out—at least partly. Because I don't want you to walk away. I don't want you thinking that you ever have to be alone." I knew I was baring my soul to the second person in my life. "I love you, Kincaid. I didn't mean to fall so fast. I don't want you to go away."

Kincaid's eyes widened, and Ronin let out a curse. "Why do you seem so surprised? I love you too, you asshole."

That made me laugh and close my eyes. "You know you're much more romantic when you're not angry," I said dryly to my husband.

Ronin shrugged. "Kincaid makes me angry, but in a good way."

"I don't understand the two of you." Kincaid looked between us. "I don't understand how you can be so open."

"I'm not," I answered. "Not to everybody. You know I've been through enough that it's not easy for me to trust. But, sometimes, people make it easy. You're one of those. Now, I don't know what's going to happen years from now, but I do know that I want you with us. Somehow. Will you take that chance?"

Ronin moved forward then and brushed his knuckles across Kincaid's bearded cheek. "Please take that chance. I lost you before. I don't want to do it again. You know Julia is our center. And she can be *our* center, not just mine. Please."

"I'm not a perfect man. I have a lot of faults, and am going to make a lot of mistakes," Kincaid said.

"And you think I'm perfect?" Ronin asked, a brow raised.

"I think that I hurt you before, and I don't want to do it again," Kincaid whispered.

"Then don't," Ronin said simply.

Kincaid sucked in a breath, then ran his hand over his red hair. For a moment, I was afraid he was going to walk away again, leaving us shattered. I knew I would always have Ronin, but there would be something missing now if we lost Kincaid. Something we hadn't known we needed.

"I love you two so much. I didn't mean to fall and get hurt on the way down, but damn it. I don't want to go anywhere. So, if you'll have a broken man who makes a lot of mistakes and doesn't know what he's doing, I'm in."

Tears fell, and then I reached out and kissed Kincaid hard on the mouth before he moved to kiss Ronin, and then I had to kiss my husband. The three of us held one another, tears falling freely down my cheeks as my men wiped them away.

I leaned into them, captured by their gazes, covered in their scents and secure in their arms, and I knew that life wouldn't be easy. The world might not understand exactly who we were and the choices we made, but their opinions and stances didn't matter in the end. What did were the two people in my arms, and whatever family we made in the future. That life was full of choices and moments of understanding, and I held the two people close that knew every ounce of me to the very depths of my soul.

I had been happy, had found my forever, and then I was blessed again with a forever wrapped in two.

* * * *

Also from 1001 Dark Nights and Carrie Ann Ryan, discover Taken With You, Ashes to Ink, Inked Nights, Wicked Wolf, Hidden Ink, and Adoring Ink.

Sign up for the 1001 Dark Nights Newsletter
and be entered to win a Tiffany Key necklace.

There's a contest every month!

Go to www.1001DarkNights.com to subscribe.

**As a bonus, all subscribers can download
FIVE FREE exclusive books!**

Discover 1001 Dark Nights Collection Eight

DRAGON REVEALED by Donna Grant
A Dragon Kings Novella

CAPTURED IN INK by Carrie Ann Ryan
A Montgomery Ink: Boulder Novella

SECURING JANE by Susan Stoker
A SEAL of Protection: Legacy Series Novella

WILD WIND by Kristen Ashley
A Chaos Novella

DARE TO TEASE by Carly Phillips
A Dare Nation Novella

VAMPIRE by Rebecca Zanetti
A Dark Protectors/Rebels Novella

MAFIA KING by Rachel Van Dyken
A Mafia Royals Novella

THE GRAVEDIGGER'S SON by Darynda Jones
A Charley Davidson Novella

FINALE by Skye Warren
A North Security Novella

MEMORIES OF YOU by J. Kenner
A Stark Securities Novella

SLAYED BY DARKNESS by Alexandra Ivy
A Guardians of Eternity Novella

TREASURED by Lexi Blake
A Masters and Mercenaries Novella

THE DAREDEVIL by Dylan Allen
A Rivers Wilde Novella

BOND OF DESTINY by Larissa Ione
A Demonica Novella

THE CLOSE-UP by Kennedy Ryan
A Hollywood Renaissance Novella

MORE THAN POSSESS YOU by Shayla Black
A More Than Words Novella

HAUNTED HOUSE by Heather Graham
A Krewe of Hunters Novella

MAN FOR ME by Laurelin Paige
A Man In Charge Novella

THE RHYTHM METHOD by Kylie Scott
A Stage Dive Novella

JONAH BENNETT by Tijan
A Bennett Mafia Novella

CHANGE WITH ME by Kristen Proby
A With Me In Seattle Novella

THE DARKEST DESTINY by Gena Showalter
A Lords of the Underworld Novella

Also from Blue Box Press

THE LAST TIARA by M.J. Rose

THE CROWN OF GILDED BONES by Jennifer L. Armentrout
A Blood and Ash Novel

THE MISSING SISTER by Lucinda Riley

Discover More Carrie Ann Ryan

Taken With You
A Fractured Connections Novella

From *New York Times* and *USA Today* bestselling author Carrie Ann Ryan comes a new story in her Fractured Connections series…

It all started at a wedding. Beckham didn't mean to dance with Meadow. And he really didn't mean to kiss her. But now, she's the only thing on his mind. And when it all comes down to it, she's the only person he can't have.

He'll just have to stay away from her, no matter how hard they're pulled together.

Running away from her friend's wedding isn't the best way to keep the gossip at bay. But falling for the mysterious and gorgeous bartender at her friends' bar will only make it worse. Beckham has his secrets, and she refuses to pry.

Once burned, twice kicked down, and never allowed to get up again. Yet taking a chance with him might be the only choice she has. And the only one she wants.

**For fans of Carrie Ann's Fractured Connections series, Taken With You is book four in that series.

* * * *

Ashes to Ink
A Montgomery Ink: Colorado Springs Novella

Back in Denver, Abby lost everything she ever loved, except for her daughter, the one memory she has left of the man she loved and lost. Now, she's moved next to the Montgomerys in Colorado Springs, leaving her past behind to start her new life.

One step at a time.

Ryan is the newest tattoo artist at Montgomery Ink Too and knows the others are curious about his secrets. But he's not ready to tell them.

Not yet. That is…until he meets Abby.

Abby and Ryan thought they had their own paths, ones that had nothing to do with one another. Then…they took a chance.

On each other.

One night at a time.

* * * *

Inked Nights
A Montgomery Ink Novella

Tattoo artist, Derek Hawkins knows the rules:
  One night a month.
  No last names.
  No promises.

Olivia Madison has her own rules:
  Don't fall in love.
  No commitment.
  Never tell Derek the truth.

When their worlds crash into each other however, Derek and Olivia will have to face what they fought to ignore as well as the connection they tried to forget.

* * * *

Adoring Ink
A Montgomery Ink Novella

Holly Rose fell in love with a Montgomery, but left him when he couldn't love her back. She might have been the one to break the ties and ensure her ex's happy ending, but now Holly's afraid she's missed out on more than a chance at forever. Though she's always been the dependable good girl, she's ready to take a leap of faith and embark on the journey of a lifetime.

Brody Deacon loves ink, women, fast cars, and living life like there's no tomorrow. The thing is, he doesn't know if he *has* a tomorrow at all. When he sees Holly, he's not only intrigued, he also hears the warnings of danger in his head. She's too sweet, too innocent, and way too special for him. But when Holly asks him to help her grab the bull by the horns, he can't help but go all in.

As they explore Holly's bucket list and their own desires, Brody will have to make sure he doesn't fall too hard and too fast. Sometimes, people think happily ever afters don't happen for everyone, and Brody will have to face his demons and tell Holly the truth of what it means to truly live life to the fullest…even when they're both running out of time.

* * * *

Hidden Ink
A Montgomery Ink Novella

The Montgomery Ink series continues with the long-awaited romance between the café owner next door and the tattoo artist who's loved her from afar.

Hailey Monroe knows the world isn't always fair, but she's picked herself up from the ashes once before and if she needs to, she'll do it again. It's been years since she first spotted the tattoo artist with a scowl that made her heart skip a beat, but now she's finally gained the courage to approach him. Only it won't be about what their future could bring, but how to finish healing the scars from her past.

Sloane Gordon lived through the worst kinds of hell yet the temptation next door sends him to another level. He's kept his distance because he knows what kind of man he is versus what kind of man Hailey needs. When she comes to him with a proposition that sends his mind whirling and his soul shattering, he'll do everything in his power to protect the woman he cares for and the secrets he's been forced to keep.

* * * *

Wicked Wolf
A Redwood Pack Novella

The war between the Redwood Pack and the Centrals is one of wolf legend. Gina Eaton lost both of her parents when a member of their Pack betrayed them. Adopted by the Alpha of the Pack as a child, Gina grew up within the royal family to become an enforcer and protector of her den. She's always known fate can be a tricky and deceitful entity, but when she finds the one man that could be her mate, she might throw caution to the wind and follow the path set out for her, rather than forging one of her own.

Quinn Weston's mate walked out on him five years ago, severing their bond in the most brutal fashion. She not only left him a shattered shadow of himself, but their newborn son as well. Now, as the lieutenant of the Talon Pack's Alpha, he puts his whole being into two things: the safety of his Pack and his son.

When the two Alphas put Gina and Quinn together to find a way to ensure their treaties remain strong, fate has a plan of its own. Neither knows what will come of the Pack's alliance, let alone one between the two of them. The past paved their paths in blood and heartache, but it will take the strength of a promise and iron will to find their future.

Inked Nights

A Montgomery Ink Novella
By Carrie Ann Ryan

From *New York Times* and *USA Today* bestselling author Carrie Ann Ryan comes a new story in her Montgomery Ink series…

Tattoo artist, Derek Hawkins knows the rules:
   One night a month.
   No last names.
   No promises.

Olivia Madison has her own rules:
   Don't fall in love.
   No commitment.
   Never tell Derek the truth.

When their worlds crash into each other however, Derek and Olivia will have to face what they fought to ignore as well as the connection they tried to forget.

* * * *

Pebbled flesh.
Quick intakes of breath.
Long sighs turning to moans.
That's what awaited Olivia Madison, and she knew it. She'd always known it. She'd rake her fingernails down his back, arch into him, and let herself be taken in the most primal way. And then she'd walk away again without looking back. They'd have a drink. They'd fuck. They'd keep it to only those details. There would be no last names, no promises. Exactly how they wanted it. And in a month, they'd do it again.

It was her thrill, her deepest secret.

Well, not her *deepest*, but the only one she could face.

Just one more time. That's what Olivia had told herself last month, and yet, she knew she would be back for more. She'd always be back for more when it came to him.

Because that was how it was, and she wasn't sure it would ever change. She wasn't sure she needed it to change. Wasn't sure she *wanted* it to change.

But she was going to push those thoughts from her mind. Because tonight was about one thing. Hot, unadulterated sex. At least that's what she kept telling herself. Because there was no way that Olivia was going to fall for the man she didn't know. She might know his body just as much as he knew hers, but that was it.

She didn't even know what his favorite drink was. She swore he ordered a different one each time they were out together just to throw her off. She'd found herself doing the same, but maybe not for the same reasons. She just liked variety, liked knowing that she didn't have to commit to something as simple as a drink.

The only commitment she allowed herself was one night a month with a man named *D*. He knew her as *O*.

And every time he called her that, there was a little laughter in his eyes because he had indeed given her a few *O*s along the way.

She mentally rolled her eyes at the horrendous joke and took a sip of her lemon drop martini. Tonight, she'd wanted something extra sweet to get the bitter taste of regret out of her mouth. For some reason, this night felt different than previous months. Maybe she was just getting old, or the fragile relationship she had with her stranger was getting stale, but either way, she felt like this might be the last one. And maybe it needed to be.

Having sex with a stranger with no promises and no strings once a month for as long as it had been going on seemed crazy and a little as if she were playing with fire. She often wondered what the manager or bartender at this hotel thought of them. Because this wasn't the first time she'd seen the same guy behind the bar, wasn't even the first time she'd seen the concierge.

Olivia wasn't the one who booked the hotel room; that had always been the job of the other person in this strange relationship.

She just had to show up at the same time every month, sip her drink, and wait. And the thrill of that set her on edge. She knew it was wrong, knew she was consistently making the same mistakes, but she didn't care, not when it came to him. And perhaps that was the greatest mistake of all.

About Carrie Ann Ryan

Carrie Ann Ryan is the *New York Times* and *USA Today* bestselling author of contemporary, paranormal, and young adult romance. Her works include the Montgomery Ink, Redwood Pack, Fractured Connections, and Elements of Five series, which have sold over 3.0 million books worldwide. She started writing while in graduate school for her advanced degree in chemistry and hasn't stopped since. Carrie Ann has written over seventy-five novels and novellas with more in the works. When she's not losing herself in her emotional and action-packed worlds, she's reading as much as she can while wrangling her clowder of cats who have more followers than she does.

www.CarrieAnnRyan.com

Discover More 1001 Dark Nights

COLLECTION ONE
FOREVER WICKED by Shayla Black ~ CRIMSON TWILIGHT by Heather Graham ~ CAPTURED IN SURRENDER by Liliana Hart ~ SILENT BITE: A SCANGUARDS WEDDING by Tina Folsom ~ DUNGEON GAMES by Lexi Blake ~ AZAGOTH by Larissa Ione ~ NEED YOU NOW by Lisa Renee Jones ~ SHOW ME, BABY by Cherise Sinclair~ ROPED IN by Lorelei James ~ TEMPTED BY MIDNIGHT by Lara Adrian ~ THE FLAME by Christopher Rice ~ CARESS OF DARKNESS by Julie Kenner

COLLECTION TWO
WICKED WOLF by Carrie Ann Ryan ~ WHEN IRISH EYES ARE HAUNTING by Heather Graham ~ EASY WITH YOU by Kristen Proby ~ MASTER OF FREEDOM by Cherise Sinclair ~ CARESS OF PLEASURE by Julie Kenner ~ ADORED by Lexi Blake ~ HADES by Larissa Ione ~ RAVAGED by Elisabeth Naughton ~ DREAM OF YOU by Jennifer L. Armentrout ~ STRIPPED DOWN by Lorelei James ~ RAGE/KILLIAN by Alexandra Ivy/Laura Wright ~ DRAGON KING by Donna Grant ~ PURE WICKED by Shayla Black ~ HARD AS STEEL by Laura Kaye ~ STROKE OF MIDNIGHT by Lara Adrian ~ ALL HALLOWS EVE by Heather Graham ~ KISS THE FLAME by Christopher Rice~ DARING HER LOVE by Melissa Foster ~ TEASED by Rebecca Zanetti ~ THE PROMISE OF SURRENDER by Liliana Hart

COLLECTION THREE
HIDDEN INK by Carrie Ann Ryan ~ BLOOD ON THE BAYOU by Heather Graham ~ SEARCHING FOR MINE by Jennifer Probst ~ DANCE OF DESIRE by Christopher Rice ~ ROUGH RHYTHM by Tessa Bailey ~ DEVOTED by Lexi Blake ~ Z by Larissa Ione ~ FALLING UNDER YOU by Laurelin Paige ~ EASY FOR KEEPS by Kristen Proby ~ UNCHAINED by Elisabeth Naughton ~ HARD TO SERVE by Laura Kaye ~ DRAGON FEVER by Donna Grant ~ KAYDEN/SIMON by Alexandra Ivy/Laura Wright ~ STRUNG UP by Lorelei James ~ MIDNIGHT UNTAMED by Lara Adrian ~ TRICKED

On Behalf of 1001 Dark Nights,

Liz Berry, M.J. Rose, and Jillian Stein would like to thank ~

Steve Berry
Doug Scofield
Benjamin Stein
Kim Guidroz
Social Butterfly PR
Ashley Wells
Asha Hossain
Chris Graham
Chelle Olson
Kasi Alexander
Jessica Johns
Dylan Stockton
Richard Blake
and Simon Lipskar